Henry P. Westlake

The New Kingdom

Henry P. Westlake

The New Kingdom

ISBN/EAN: 9783337183950

Printed in Europe, USA, Canada, Australia, Japan

Cover: Foto ©Andreas Hilbeck / pixelio.de

More available books at **www.hansebooks.com**

THE

NEW KINGDOM,

A TREATISE ON

THE FALL OF MAN

AND THE

IDENTITY OF THE SERPENT,

THE EXTENT OF THE FLOOD

AND

THE PROBABLE END OF TIME.

BY H. P. WESTLAKE.

ST. LOUIS, MO.
WESTLAKE-SMITH ENG. CO., PUBLISHERS,
1892.

PREFACE.

When this book was commenced there was existing in some of the periodicals a lively controversy regarding the utterances of a rather noted infidel. These writings were designed as a few short contributions on the same subject.

But on beginning and proceeding for a time, it seemed to expand and grow into such vast proportions, and to become of such vital importance, as to require a more extended and careful consideration. Hence the production of this volume.

Only a few things of the infinite many, have been touched upon at all, and they in the briefest manner possible.

The chief object has been to give conclusions and deductions, rather than to go into a laborious proof of their correctness.

That the reader should be induced to free himself from the bias of dogmas, from the incubus of traditions, and with untrammeled, unprejudiced mind to seek for the very truth itself, is all that is aimed at by

THE AUTHOR.

CONTENTS.

CHAPTER I.

SECTARIAN INFLUENCE INJURIOUS.

This appears to be a time of general inquiry into the truths of Christianity, and the justification for the numerous branches. that are attached to the parent stem.

It is a matter of regret that an infidel, one who believes in nothing spiritual, nothing in the Book of books, who derides and scorns that which has stood the test of centuries and been the beacon and the guiding star of millions of earth's good and great, should be the inciting cause to this lively interest.

We must admit that it is natural to humanity to defend from attack that which it holds as not only true but sacred. But repelling assaults or even persecution, is not consistent with the teaching of Christianity. Meekness, submission, endurance without resistance, are its chief tenets.

And yet at the first blast from the

challenging trumpet of this really harmless being, the ministers of a peaceful Prince put on their armor and are ready to meet or to force the deadly conflict, that they must feel can result in no good to man, nor in honor to God.

They know that the bright intellect is prostituted for money; they know that a mind so clear and strong of comprehension as his, so vivid in imagery, so keen in the sharp thrusts of irony cannot possibly be a dullard to the inspired teachings of the Bible; cannot be blind and irresponsive to the supreme grandeur of creation.

How can they meet the attack of ridicule? How can they dull or turn aside the point of sarcasm? How rebut and neutralize the meaningless ranting of the unbeliever? Surely not by contending with his own weapons. And why use arguments when nothing is opposing? Why desecrate the good and the beautiful by placing them in reach of the tongue that touches only to pollute, whose feet would tramp pearls in the mire.

"To fight the devil with fire" sounds logical, but it is a proverb that has age without wisdom.

Strife encourages strife; contention begets stubbornness, often anger, and not infrequently crystalizes doubt into confirmed unbelief.

What then is the method that would probably prove most productive of good? Naturally but two ways remain; give the reason of your own belief in the clearest, most convincing, yet briefest possible manner; and the other, live your belief; let your light shine that all may see; have charity to man, a clean life, reverence for everything pure, and a reaching upward to the source of all purity.

These two should constitute the only weapons of warfare with infidelity; and even they might never convince a single infidel. But should they not, they could not fail at least to be of vast advantage to others, and, which is of much more importance, sacred things would not be desecrated.

It cannot be denied by the most zealous

believers that there are ample grounds for adverse criticism, not of the Christian doctrine itself, but of the almost numberless sects and schisms that exist throughout the world; all founded on the same Rock, all drawing their articles of faith from the same unalterable book of truth, yet diametrically opposite on vital points, contending and clashing one with another, and condemning to perdition with the hearty earnestness of the evil one himself.

What a sharp weapon of attack is put in the hands of the skilled antagonist by the unrelenting contest over baptism, the Eucharist, purgatory, predestination, eternal punishment, and even reaching down to the minor points of church decorum.

The infidel can reasonably ask why should there exist such grave doubts on these points where one would expect the clearest light? Why is there any obscurity as to the proper method of administering the rite of baptism, and of partaking of the Lord's supper?

Why should one have a choice as to free

will or predestination? Is only one way right? And if only one, which is the one? And why does not our Bible clearly settle these several points of endless and bitter contests between the different Christian sects?

There is one other and most effective weapon of infidelity, effective, because believed in by nearly all Christians, and that is the doctrine that a merciful Being elects a few to bliss, and condemns the unnumbered legions to endless torments; a Being that not only created, but that foreknew all things from the beginning.

Taking into consideration all the points of weakness in the armor of the modern churchmen, it is not surprising that the attacks of enemies are frequent and bold, while the defence can not be otherwise than weak, rambling and spiritless.

As an expounder of views that will doubtless seem wild, and, it may be, without warrant of authority from any source, I know that I tread on untried, dangerous ground.

But I pray patience and serious reflection.

There is a spirit of unrest in the land. Many ministers of high repute, churchmen of national renown, are disavowing the creeds of their churches, creeds that they have clung to through years and years of prayer and preaching, and now are apparently wandering aimless, guideless in a wilderness of doubt.

It is too evidently true that the creeds of the different churches are based on a more or less forced interpretation of the Scriptures; forced, inasmuch as they do not perfectly harmonize with all the Scriptures as an entirety.

Each sect, having established its faith on some particular doctrinal point, immediately expounds the Bible as agreeing perfectly therewith. The Lutheran and the Calvinist draw their antagonizing creeds from the same teacher. The believer in a burning hell as well as the believer in universal redemption, brings the Bible in as clearly authorizing his creed.

Is there not something radically wrong in the common method of Scripture study?

Or is it because of having been reared from childhood within the influence of these sectarian differences, the mind never gets beyond using them as a gauge in scriptural interpretation?

This is a grave error. We should investigate and seek after the truth for the truth's sake alone, and without desiring or trying in the least to find support for any particular bias or belief. Such an investigation is not only possible, but it is the only kind that can ever result in the solution of these disputed points.

There surely can be some exposition of the providence of God toward man that is consistent with all parts of his revealed word; an exposition that would, we feel assured, not only dispel all doubts, all disputes and bickerings, but would fill us with awe and wonder at the grandeur of the great plan whose conception was before time began, its consummation when time ends.

CHAPTER II.

WHAT IS REQUIRED IN SEARCHING THE SCRIPT-URES.

We accept the Bible as the book of God; a book that, although it has been in the hands of man for nearly twenty centuries, is substantially true in all its parts; a book that reveals the works of His creation, and the laws that he requires us to observe; gives the account of man's fall and his continuous disobedience, the penalties so often inflicted, and the plan of his final redemption; the rise and fall of mighty nations of antiquity; and in general, a concise statement of the most important events in the world's history down to the coming of the Savior. A period that would otherwise have remained in almost impenetrable obscurity.

It is worthy of continued remembrance that from the beginning to the end of this sacred volume, there is one thing impera-

tively demanded of mankind; one require-
ment standing pre-eminent to all others, and
that is, entire belief in its statements, a cre-
dence.unlimited, a trust unclouded with a
doubt. Adam doubted God's word and fell:
the antediluvians had no faith in the oft given
warnings, and the flood came; the Jews in
the wilderness, and afterwards, endured the
penalties of unbelief.

On the other hand, most signal blessing
always attended faith. Abraham was blessed
beyond all the children of men, not only in
worldly wealth, but in promises for the future
that did not fail.

When the Son came, faith in his word,
the simple belief that he was the Son of God,
wrought miracles, healed the sick, even raised
the dead to life again.

It is the Christian's present strength and
his hope for the future. It is the one chief
and only support of the church of Christ, as
without it there is no Christianity.

In order therefore to study the Scriptures
in a proper manner, we must do so in a faith
that is as limitless as the power of God;

doubting nothing, whether it is understood by us, or not understood; never for a moment questioning the word of that Being who rules the universe, and who is infinite in all his attributes.

We are not required to believe that the Bible is a book inspired in all its parts. A large portion of the Old Testament is devoted to a history of the Jewish nation, of its various rulers, and of its many bloody, devastating wars with other nations. We can judge of the accuracy of these by reflecting upon the eminence and reputed truthfulness of the different authors or compilers, the care with . which their writings were kept and handed down to succeeding generations, and the invariableness of their verification by contemporaneous histories whenever the same events were recorded.

It may be also admitted that owing to its numerous translations into other languages errors have crept in, but none of a character to in the least change the sense, or in any way detract from its common repute of being strictly true.

The New Testament can safely be taken as inspired. That is to say, all of the writers, as is admitted by all Christians, were possessed of the Holy Ghost, as was promised them by the Savior; and we need have no fear that any statement made by them, any revelation of spiritual import, any doctrinal points stated, or rules of life prescribed, was not given under divine direction and binding upon all.

We should also bear in mind that no more is ever stated than the case required.

There are no reasons given, no minute details of events are recorded, but only the abrupt, positive assertion of facts, or proclaiming of laws, that are and of necessity must be true and binding without proof.

It will be worse than profitless to investigate the Bible records while possessed of an inclination to doubt, a disposition to quibble and criticize.

It tells us that the world and all that therein is, and the sun, and the moon, and stars, were all created in six days.

Researches in the fossiliferous rocks of

the earth demonstrate the fact that it was in
a process of construction for unnumbered
cycles.   As the word and the works of God
cannot disagree, we conclude at once that by
six days was not meant six revolutions of the
earth, but six vast periods of millions of years
each, during which he was preparing the
earth for man's occupancy.

Although the fossils, like a book with
only a torn leaf here and there remaining,
bear evidence of an order in creation somewhat similar to that given in the Bible; still
no explanation is needed where the six days
are evidently meant as typical. The Lord
had divided his work of preparing man's
future home into six periods; he required
man to forever commemorate it by resting
on the seventh of his days.

The account of the fall of man is given
with equal terseness; but what would avail
anything more elaborate?   It was sufficient
to narrate the circumstances that have
especial bearing on and lead up to the great
catastrophe—the existence of the tree, the
command against eating its fruit, the viola-

tion of the command and the penalty imposed.

The same brevity of narration, the same meagreness of detail, is ever found in the Bible. No more is said than is necessary to impress the meaning with sufficient emphasis.

We can rest in the assurance that whatever is obscure and mysterious is either designed to be so, or the fault lies with us; that whatever seems contradictory is only so in seeming, as there can be no contradiction.

The Bible was given us as a teacher and a guide, and inculcates no errors.

As we have all the riches of its contents open before us, the narration of events from before the creation to the coming of Christ, as well as the prophecies reaching forward to the end of the world, it would seem eminently consistent with the intelligence and the reasoning powers we possess, and with the spirit of inquiry with which we are endowed, to read and meditate on the grand revelations of both the Bible and nature, and to reflect, compare, and construct from the evidence before us.

How profoundly moved we are when we look backward through and beyond the dim past; forward to the bright realms of assured eternity; down at the dark recesses of earth; its rivers of poured out blood; its crimes and oppressions; its mocking of all that is good; its blasphemies and corruptions that, from the creation of man, have befouled the pure air of heaven.

Then we turn upward the reflective gaze to the sun and its planets, and to the shining worlds beyond; those far-away, gleaming, sparkling gems of light, those mere points of scintillating brilliancy, millions on millions in number and billions of miles away, which we know are in reality gigantic, glowing suns, the central ruling powers of encircling planetary systems.

We see and are filled with awe. All things in nature are incomprehensible in magnitude, unerring in operation, whether it be in creating and controlling systems of worlds, or in bringing up from the mould of the earth the beautiful, fragrant little flower.

All show attributes beyond our comprehension, infinite in all things, in wisdom and power, and in beauty and magnitude of design as in perfection of execution. Seeing only infinite wisdom in all things else, can we for a moment suppose that there was not design, a fixed purpose in creating the earth, and in placing innocent, weak man in the garden of Eden, and subjecting him to a dual temptation? We cannot doubt there was. What that design was and is we can only know in the great hereafter. But we can be quite certain of one thing, yea, of two—when the great work is finished there will be legions more of angels to glorify God, and not one additional sufferer of eternal torment.

We cannot reconcile eternal punishment with infinite mercy. There is not the least doubt that the plan of salvation as adopted, was the one that perfectly secured the Divine aim, and at the same time was in strict accord with his mercy.

Before enlarging upon the subject of man's relation to God in his creation, and in his present and future state, we will proceed to a consideration of the word and works of

God, as impressing us with the conviction that there is, and has been from the beginning, some grand scheme of heaven's great King, of which our existence forms but a part, and that our creation, with all the subsequent incidents of the temptation and death penalty, the coming of the Savior and restoration to life, are only portions of this foreordained, unalterable design that will end with time in a grand consummation.

The revelations on this subject are abundant, and in some respects most clear, in others obscure. Still there is enough to form conclusions that seem not only warranted by the Bible but are consistent with the divine attributes.

CHAPTER III.

FALL OF SATAN AND DESTRUCTION OF HIS KINGDOM.

The Devil and his angels were once servants of the Most High ; angels of light, and obedient to His will.

We cannot comprehend the possibility of their desiring to rebel, believing, as we do, in the perfect purity of the angel nature ; and still less can we understand how they could, in the least degree, expect to war successfully against infinite power. Though the Bible, from beginning to end, abounds in angel history, we know nothing of their real appearance, their individuality, as they are spirits, invisible and indescribable to us.

We only know that there are two kinds, good and bad ; the former, as the ministers of God, doing His will in heaven and on earth; with the power to annihilate, and the power to create even great worlds, and swing

them forth on their orbits in illimitable
space ; the latter to do evil continually, and
strive to undo the works of the good.   We
infer that there are degrees of angel power
and authority.   Gabriel stands continuously
before God.   Michael and his hosts had
charge of the Hebrews.   There was a Prince
for Persia, one for Grecia, and probably one
for each of the other kingdoms of the world;
and with each prince there were no doubt
hosts of assistant angels, each doing his
share of the work assigned.   Against these
were evil angels opposed.   An angel told
Daniel that he had been delayed in Persia
for one and twenty days in a struggle with
the evil prince of that nation, but Michael,
one of the chief princes, coming to his assistance, they succeeded in subduing the
evil prince ; that the Prince of Grecia would
come on his leaving, as he had to return and
again fight the prince of Persia ; that he had
assisted Darius, the Mede, during the first
year of his reign ; and the things he was
about to tell Daniel were known only to
himself and Michael.

We have not the least reason to suppose that there is another world in the universe like ours ; a world in a state of transition from mortality to immortality ; a world reeking in crime, groaning under the ills of the flesh, seething and bubbling in corruption; and where the angels of heaven and hell are fighting their great battles over the souls of the elect of God. We know of but one sinful world ; we know of only one rebellion in heaven. We conclude, therefore, with certainty that all the rest of God's creation is pure and undefiled ; that all those bright orbs that nightly illume the sky, reaching beyond our system into the dark, etherial blue of fathomless space, are the heavenly abodes of angels, and archangels, and spirits of God, that know not sin.

Is it not then more than probable that at some past time our planetary system was a heavenly kingdom, even the kingdom of Satan himself ?

The Scriptures indicate this, and on its admission as a fact, the providence of God towards man, in his creation, and in his ultimate redemption and location on earth, appeals to our intelligence as most grand and God-like in all its parts.

Satan, in the zenith of his glory, was a mighty prince before the Lord, having dominion over principalities and powers, and with legions of angels to do his will.

His was the august imperialism to sit enthroned in gorgeous state on a vast globe of liquid radiancy, surrounded with his great armies of winged angels, who, obedient to his every command, sped, as the lightnings flash, with messages of greeting or command, to the waiting hosts on Venus, or Earth, or away to Saturn, or Jupiter, or further Neptune --- those worlds of angelic abode, moving, with silent grandeur, round about the throne of their great prince.

The human mind cannot conceive the immensity of power, nor the splendor of the realms, of these Chiefs of the hosts of the Lord.

But with power eventually came pride, and with pride, ambition --- a vaulting ambition, that dared the power of heaven's great King.

" And there appeared a wonder in heaven, and behold a great red dragon having seven heads and ten horns, and seven crowns upon his heads."

" And his tail drew the third part of the stars of heaven and did cast them to the earth."

" And there was war in heaven. Michael and his angels fought against the dragon, and the dragon fought and his angels, and prevailed not; neither was their place found any more in heaven."

" And the great dragon was cast out, that old Serpent called the Devil, and Satan, which deceiveth the whole world; he was cast out into the earth and his angels were cast out with him." ''He was seen to fall as lightning from heaven."

The rebellion seems to have spread beyond Satan's own dominion, as he drew with him " the third part of the stars of heaven."

And how fearful was the defeat, as driven from heaven's ramparts by the thunder bolts of the great Jehovah, he was hurled back again to his own kingdom, broken, crushed, and held with the chains of Omnipotence.

And in his fall he may have struck an intervening world and crushed it into the fragmentary orbs of Juno, Ceres and their scores of companion asteroids.

Perhaps the just anger of God did not stop there, but the vials of his wrath were poured out on all of Satan's great domain.

The sun, his seat of empire, may have trembled and rocked to its very center, and then burst forth into great mountain billows of seething flame, throwing out millions of tongues of liquid fire, roaring, darting to and fro, for thousands upon thousands of miles; and the earth, and the moon, and all the planets and their satellites, may have reeled to and fro under the fierce anger of God.

And earthquakes came, with thunders and fearful roarings, until all barriers gave way, and each and every celestial world was deluged with seas of consuming fire, and all the fair mounts were melted down, and the lovely vales were pits of destruction.

The flames of their burning for long ages ascended to heaven as the odor of incense.

But a change came; the brightness that once filled all the firmament of heaven and made perpetual day grew less, and still less; the gloom of a long night drew near; the expurging fires are all out; the sun's sullen red gives no light, and the planets, now dark in their ruin, wrecked, and utterly devastated, swing for ages upon ages, through a rayless night—a night rayless and appalling—where no gleam from friendly star ever entered; where the awful silence was never broken by rustling wings, or if broken at all, 'twas by the moans and mutterings of the fallen angels, those shadows of evil, shorn of power and chained, except for a brief period, unto the day of Judgment and eternal condemnation.

There approaches now another epoch in the decreed plans of God, and the earth is taken as the theatre of action. Chaos still reigned. "The earth was without form and void, and darkness was upon the face of the deep, and the spirit of God moved upon the face of the waters."

"And God said, 'Let there be light,' and there was light," and time began.

"Let the waters be gathered together unto one place and let the dry land appear, and it was so."

"Let the earth bring forth grass and trees bearing fruit."

"Let the waters bring forth abundantly the moving creatures that have life, and fowls that may fly above the earth."

"Let the earth bring forth the living creature, cattle and creeping things, and beasts of the earth," "and it was so, and all were good."

But many millions of years had passed before all things were finished.

CHAPTER IV.

RESTORATION OF THE EARTH FOR MAN'S HABITATION.

A wrecked word was to be made a dwelling place suitable for the highest types of animal and vegetable life, and made, not by the uplifted hand of omnipotent power, but by agencies created for the especial purpose.

The only land, were yet smoking mountains of granite, lava and scoriæ ; the only water, steaming oceans like dead seas ; the only atmosphere, gases noxious as the breath of a furnace.

But the ages passed, and the sun, and vapors, and beating waves, eroded and washed down the hard granite and the scoriæ, forming sloping shores and cozy nooks; and there was placed the first of the new creation, the sea moss. In appearance it differed little from the dead matter beside it.

But it possessed that which nothing else on the whole earth possessed --- life ; and, with life, the power to increase and multiply.

There it lived, the first and lowest of material life ; lived and increased abundantly, nourished by water and air and mineral detritus.

Then came others of the same family, confervæ and fungi, all working together in laying the foundation for other and higher orders of vegetable life.

Another kind of life was next created and placed with the primeval one, and that was the animal. The vegetable was required to sustain the animal, the latter having no power to assimilate matter that had not first been acted on by vegetable organization --- this last acting as the connecting link between dead matter and spirit life.

These two were the agents that reconstructed the world ; the one on land, the other in the sea.

Other ages passed, thousands of ages, and the great work continued.

The smallest of animal workers, millions

of whom could gather in the shade of a single fungus, protozoans, polypes, foraminiferæ, built great mountains of limestone, and even displaced the mighty ocean.

On land the work performed was equally as grand. The world's combustion had left the air heavy with carbonic acid. Although the mountain and reef-builders had used it freely in making carbonate of lime, and a much greater quantity had been taken up by vegetation, and stored away for future use, deep in the earth, in great beds of coal, enough was yet left for continuous service, for the world was covered with herbs and grasses and trees bearing fruit.

The animal kingdom had kept in a parallel line of progress.

The waters swarmed with living creatures ; and the dry land was covered, and the air filled, with species, families and orders of animated nature in never-ending variety.

On reading the history of creation, as written in the rocks, we are filled with wonder, not only at the immensity of time it undoubtedly covers, but at the thousands of

most wonderful objects it discloses. Everything created in those far-away times, from
the very smallest to the most gigantic, was
perfect, and often exquisitely beautiful.

The animal kingdom is generally divided
into four grand divisions --- the mollusks, radiates, articulates and vertebrates. These
divisions only embrace the higher orders of
animal life, as there are thousands of species
too minute for investigation, and go under
some general classification, as protozoans,
infusoria, insectivera, baccili and the like.

The first three of the four grand divisions furnish by far the most sub-divisions of
orders, families and species, each distinctively
different from all the others ; but it is only
to the last division, the vertebrates, that all
the higher types of animals belong. Fishes,
reptiles, mammals and birds are but modifications of one chief design --- an internal
bony structure, with vertebrates entire or in
part, and with processes for locomotion,
changed in all the ways necessary to exactly
suit the location and the wants of each animal.

The fins of the fish, the legs of the quad-
ruped, the legs and wings of the bird, are
all modifications of one prototype, modifications so evidently designed by supreme intelligence that none can doubt.

This using one original mould, as it were,
to shape a thousand different forms is illus-
trated in every known species of animals, as
well as in the divisions. Take, as an example, the ancient family of Trilobites, who
flourished before the coal formations, probably twenty millions of years ago.

Remains have been found in the rocks
of more than six hundred different species
of this one family of crustaceans. Each
species belonged to the same great family,
but was as distinct from all the rest as
though it belonged to a different order.

And the same law of diversity applies to
individuals as well. Nature never repeats or
duplicates. Of all the millions of men on
earth, probably no two are exactly alike. Of
all the leaves in the forest, of all the blades
of grass, or seeds of grain, no man ever
found any two identical in every part.

The proofs are so indisputable of an intelligent, ever present, creative agency, that it would not seem possible for any one to doubt. The theory of evolution by an inherent principle or capability of matter to readjust and modify itself according to surrounding conditions, to change itself into other and higher species, orders and divisions of life, is not only absurd and utterly unworthy of consideration, but no one except an infidel can in the least degree accede to it.

The laws of nature are the laws which the Creator has made --- not made so much as determined on --- in accordance with which He Himself governs and controls all things.

The workings of nature are as secret and noiseless as the movements of a spirit. We understand nothing of all that we see ; not even concerning the motive powers of our own body. We can take it apart, as we would a piece of machinery, analyze its component parts, and number and give names ; but we have not and never will find one of its hundreds of life laboratories.

Can we understand or explain the attraction of matter? Is it a material substance? In what shape does it exist? How can it reach forth from the sun, 92,000,000 miles away, and hold and swing around itself this ponderous globe of ours as though with bands of steel?

How can the rays of the sun pass through these millions of miles of vacuum and retain their heat? How can they be icy cold on the mountain tops and glowing in the valleys?

The only explanation is that the Supreme being upholds, sustains and does all things by the power of His might, and that His power alone is the law of nature.

Diversity in the vegetable kingdom was equally as great as in the animal, although the specimens obtained are fewer in number owing to their fragile nature. But these few show divisions and subdivisions, orders and species, with distinctive differences pervading all.

And from the lowest in the scale, the sea weed and moss, to the highest of the coal age, to mosses and ferns developed into new families or orders of gigantic and beautiful trees, to calamites and conifers ; all bear evidence of an All wise designer and Creator, in perfection and beauty, and in thorough adaptation to their position and uses in creation.

In reflecting on the works of creation there is one consideration that is impressive. From the dawn of time until the present the world has been the arena of violence and carnage.

The first dwellers in the sea, the protozoans, and many families of radiates and molusca, drew nourishment from the sea weed and confervæ that grew along the shores of the ancient seas. But presently animals came equipped with carnivorous appetites and the slaughter began. And this same law of two opposing grand divisions of animal life prevailed in all subsequent creation on land and in the air, as well as in the sea. The herbivorous consuming herbs and grass and seeds and the carnivorous consuming flesh.

By this wise arrangement an equilibrium

was maintained in all three kingdoms. For the carniveri, besides being of low fecundity, were thoroughly armed with instruments of destruction, and being vicious and fierce by nature, they were a check unto themselves.

Nothing can be more interesting than a study of the huge flesh eaters of early times.

The sea had its sharks a hundred feet in length; its ganoids, from thirty to fifty feet, and clad in scaley armor nearly or quite as hard as steel and of most beautiful design.

One species had arms heavily plated and sharp pointed, a solid helmet covering its head, and a coat of mail for its body. Another had double rows of powerful teeth set in plates of solid bone that lined the entire mouth, protecting it from the shells of the mollusks it had to crush for its food.

The saurians were very numerous, as some fifty different species have been found. One species had a jointed neck ten feet long, with a head like a snake; another had a mouth that would open six feet, and great eyes nearly two feet in diameter.

But the most wonderful for that age was

a huge bat-like creature, with leathery wings twenty feet from tip to tip, and with the jaws and teeth of a saurian.

These were probably only a few of the many kinds of strange monsters that terrorized the ancient seas.

The beasts that roamed the forests and along the marshy shores were equally gigantic and terrible.

Only a few of the remains have been found, and they chiefly of saurians, varying in length from thirty to seventy-five feet. They were all flesh eaters, and must have been fearful in their strength and ferocity.

The history of the earth, as compiled from the testimony of the rocks, is commonly divided by geologists into seven great periods called ages; the Azoic, (this was the preparatory age, and was with out recognized fossils), the age of Mollusks, of Fishes, of Coal Plants, of Reptiles, of Mammals, and of Man.

Each age, in its turn, had an increase in the percentage of its peculiar fossils, a culmination and a decline. The last was that of mammals. The preceding one, that of reptiles, had declined, and the terrible saurians were disappearing. The age of mammals came in with a different and higher order of animal life, pachyderms, and other herbiverous and peaceful quadrupeds. But at the zenith of the age creatures of gigantic size roamed the earth from the equator to the Arctic circle, and grazed upon the verdant plateaus and in the dense thickets of river valleys. The mastodon, the megatherium and the glyptodon had their days, and with their decline came in other smaller but useful orders, the camel, several species of the horse, and other kinds that would be necessary for the comfort and happiness of man.

The earth was now comparatively safe and the air was pure; the soil, with its grain and fruits, was ready for the husbandman, the flocks for the shepherd, and the seventh and last age would begin.

CHAPTER V.

CREATION AND FALL OF MAN.

The fifth day of creation had ended. The earth brought forth every green thing, herbs and grasses, and trees bearing fruit. And the sea was full of every living creature that moveth, and the earth of cattle and creeping things, and the air of fowls that fly above the earth. All were now finished, and all were good.

The work had gone steadily and progressively on for millions of years. There would be long ages of quiet and peaceful growth; then would come times of violent changes, and an overwhelming of all things.

The fossil remains of the giant fishes are found crushed beneath mountains of stone, while the latter, for miles in depth, are crumpled and contorted like the leaves of a book.

At one time the temperate zone reached to near the present axis of the earth; and animals, like those now in Africa and southern Asia, lived and flourished in northern America and Europe.

Then occurred one of those collossal changes, probably by a shifting of the earth's axis, that destroyed nearly all of animal and vegetable life; and glaciers filled all the valleys, and fields of ice covered most of the eastern and western continents.

These destructive changes seem to have been, in part at least, for the purpose of renewing the existing creations, as they were always succeeded by new and higher types.

But the acme designed from the beginning had been reached at last, and the next creative act would be the chief and final one, the one for whose sake all the preceding ones had been performed. And performed for him, not so much because man himself was so superior to all the others, but because of his being the race from whom the Lord God would create, and elect, and set apart unto himself the chiefest of Princes, and hosts of angels, to reinhabit the lost kingdom of Satan.

A mighty prince of the Lord had rebelled and lost his place in heaven, and now, the mightiness in all the universe would be chosen, an emanation from God himself; and being incarnated with the flesh of the new man, would be called the Son of Man, and the Son of God, the only Son; and he would occupy the vacated place, he and the elect, with a new heaven and a new earth.

"And God said, Let us make man in our image, after our likeness, and let them have dominion over the fish of the sea, and over the fowl of the air, and over the cattle, and over all the earth, and over every creeping thing that creepeth upon the earth."

"And the Lord formed man of the dust of the ground, and breathed into his nostrils the breath of life, and man became a living soul."

"And the Lord God planted a garden eastward in Eden; and there he put the man whom he had formed. And out of the ground made the Lord God to grow every tree that is pleasant to the sight and good for food; the tree of life also in the midst of the garden, and the tree of the knowledge of good and evil. And a river went out of Eden to water the garden."

"And the Lord God took the man and put him into the garden of Eden, to dress it and to keep it. And the Lord God commanded the man, saying, 'Of every tree of the garden thou mayest freely eat; but of the tree of knowledge of good and evil thou shalt not eat of it; for in the day that thou eatest thereof thou shalt surely die."

"And the Lord God caused a deep sleep to fall upon Adam, and he slept; and he took one of his ribs and closed up the flesh instead thereof; and the rib which the Lord God had taken from man, made he a woman, and brought her unto the man."

"And Adam said; This is now bone of my bones, and flesh of my flesh; she shall be called woman, because she was taken out of man."

"Therefore shall a man leave his father and his mother and shall cleave unto his wife; and they shall be one flesh."

Now the serpent was more subtile than

any beast of the field which the Lord God had made; and he said unto the woman, "Yea, hath God said, 'Ye shall not eat of every tree of the garden.'"

And the woman said unto the serpent, "We may eat of the fruit of the trees of the garden; but of the fruit of the tree which is in the midst of the garden God hath said, ye shall not eat of it, neither shall ye touch it, lest ye die."

And the serpent said unto the woman; "Ye shall not surely die; for God doth know that in the day ye eat thereof then your eyes shall be opened and ye shall be as Gods, knowing good and evil."

And when the woman saw that the tree was good for food, and that it was pleasant to the eyes, and a tree to be desired to make one wise; she took of the fruit thereof, and did eat, and gave also unto her husband with her, and he did eat."

"And the eyes of them both were opened."

And the Lord God said unto the woman, "What is this that thou hast done?" And the woman said, "The serpent beguiled me and I did eat."

And the Lord God said unto the serpent, "Because thou hast done this, thou art cursed above all cattle and above every beast of the field; upon thy belly shalt thou go, and dust thou shalt eat all the days of thy life."

"And I wilt put enmity between thee and the woman, and between thy seed and her seed; it shalt bruise thy head, and thou shalt bruise his heel.

And unto Adam he said, "In the sweat of thy face shalt thou eat bread till thou return unto the ground, for out of it wast thou taken; for dust thou art, and unto dust shalt thou return."

And the Lord God said, "Behold the man is become one of us; to know good and evil." And now lest he put forth his hand and take also of the tree of life and eat and live forever, therefore the Lord God sent him from the garden of Eden to till the ground from where he was taken.

So he drove out the man; and he placed at the east of the gardenof Eden Cherubims and a flaming sword which turned ever way to keep the way of the tree of life.

This is the only account of the origin of man known amongst men. Only a misty tradition of the flood existed amongst the most enlightened of ancient nations two thousand years after the event. As man was created, according to the generally accepted chronology, some seventeen hundred years before the flood, and as Adam and Eve were the only ones cognizant of all its incidents, and would naturally not feel disposed to tell the particulars to their children, it is of the highest probability that at the time of the flood, even the chief act, the creation of man, was forgotten.

Noah, the chosen of God, would know, but naturally the knowledge would be confined to the servants of God, who were few in number; and their account of the works of the Lord thousands of years before, would be treated as idle dreams, and not worthy of being held as even tradition.

All the events connected with the garden of Eden demand the closest attention and most serious thought. And though the wisest of various ages of the world, and the most learned in the Scriptures in their original tongues, and the most thoroughly versed in human science, have devoted years of study to it, and written hundreds of books in elucidation, nothing is any more clear or determined than at first. While some contend that the serpent was a veritable serpent, an ophidian, a snake, a creature, though vicious and poisonous, is of the lowest order of intellect, without cunning and subtility, and in being utterly incapable of standing and moving erect, could not be abased to crawling in the dust; others, by their learned researches in dead languages, would make it apparent that there was probably some beast of the field existing at that time, similar in appearance to Adam, erect and capable of talking, who was the temper, and that he was subsequently reduced to the condition of the present quadrumanous genius, such as the orang outang, the wild man of Malay.

In regard to the penalty inflicted for eating of the forbidden fruit, nearly all men agree that it was a spiritual death; that previous to the eating man was pure, innocent, without guile, even as an angel; that immediately on eating his nature changed, he was not only disobedient to God and unfit for Paradise, but his heart, his whole being became inclined to evil, and a fit abode for the spirits of the devil.

For they contend that when the Lord made man out of the dust of the earth, and breathed into him the breath of life, and he became a living soul, that the term "living" soul meant "immortal" soul; and that consequently the only death that could be, was a spiritual death; and not a death by annihilation of the spirit, as of the body on its dying— but rather of the eternal punishment of the spirit after it had left the dead body of dust. And that this eternal punishment affected not only Adam and Eve, but also all of their descendants to the end of time; and that as the Savior did not come for four thousand years afterwards, and had not in the meantime been held up, even as the brazen serpent was in the wilderness, that the people might believe and be saved, so all the thousands, millions, billions of men, women and children that had lived and died during that long time were forever lost.

Is it not hard to believe that for a single act of disobedience on the part of Adam and Eve, not for any great and fearful crime committed, as blasphemy toward God, or defiantly worshipping devils, but for only once eating fruit that the Lord had commanded them not to eat, that they and all their descendants of thousands of generations, with a few exceptions, should be tormented day and night through all eternity?

This is not in accordance with our conception of the divine power, divine justice and divine mercy, as obtained from the Bible—so we must conclude that these interpretations are wrong, in whole or in part; and it behooves us to see if such an exposition can be given as will be consistent and harmonious in all its parts, and will do no violence to our firm convictions regarding the divine attributes.

CHAPTER VI.

THE NATURE OF THE FALL AND IDENTITY OF THE SERPENT.

We have the strongest evidence that at the time Adam was created the earth was infested with beasts of prey to a far greater extent than at this day; and we can not doubt that the forests around Eden, which was located somewhere in Asia Minor, abounded with tigers, leopards, wolves and other ferocious animals, as well as with large serpents and poisonous reptiles. A walled enclosure was necessary for man's helpless condition.

And as the forest did not yield the food necessary for his sustenance, a garden was planted, a garden of fruit-bearing trees, and possibly of wheat, lentils and herbs.

All animals were wild, and could only be tamed after long and persistent effort; and probably could not be tamed at all, as nature seems to provide the two kinds, one for the forest and persistently wild, the other for the use of man.   So cattle had to be created, and horses, sheep, goats and domestic fowls; and these were the kind brought before Adam, and by him given names.   He required these for sacrifice to the Lord, and for milk; and the domestic fowls for the eggs they yielded.   He was not permitted to eat their flesh, but their products were equally necessary for his health and comfort as were the fruits and grains.

When he was expelled from the garden he took these with him; for we read that of his two oldest sons, Cain was a tiller of the soil, and Abel was a keeper of sheep; and this, while Adam was comparatively a young man.

So Adam and Eve kept the garden of Eden and dressed it, and enjoyed the fruits provided by the Lord.

But the serpent appeared in this peaceful scene to undo the work of the Lord; the old serpent, the great red dragon, that had rebelled aga'nst Heaven, and had been cast,

he and his angels, to the earth—the beast
that, in after times, would war against the
saints, and persecute the seed of the woman
—he appeared before Eve, and with his subtility did beguile her.

The form assumed would be that of an
angel, which he was, but shaped to the view
like unto a man.

We know not the power the fallen angels
were permitted to retain, nor the forms they
took in order to deceive men, and to frus-
trate the plans of the Lord. "It came to
pass, when men began to multiply on the
face of the earth, and daughters were born
unto them, that the Sons of God saw the
daughters of men that they were fair, and
they took them wives of all which they
chose; and the Lord said: 'My spirit shall not
always strive with man, for that he also is flesh.'

"There were giants in the earth in those
days; and also after that, when the Sons of
God came in unto the daughters of men, and
they bare children to them, the same became
mighty men, which, were of old, men of
renown.

"And God saw that the wickedness of man was great in the earth, and that every imagination of the thoughts of his heart was only evil continually."

It is quite evident that the Sons of God were not of the family of Adam. He himself was never called the Son of God, so how could his sons be called by that name? And had these Sons of God been of Adam's race, in what way was it worthy of such particular mention that they should consider the daughters of men fair, and should take them wives of all which they chose? Their doing so would have been simply in accord with the divine command, "to increase and multiply and replenish the earth," and would have resulted in other sons and daughters like their first parents, Adam and Eve.

Particular stress is laid not only on the fact of this intercourse between the Sons of God and the daughters of men, but also on the important fact that their issue, their offspring, were giants, which was not the case when the sons and daughters of men intermarried.

And not only were giants the result of this remarkable intermarriage, but iniquity increased. "God saw that the wickedness of man was great in the earth, and that every imagination of the thoughts of his heart was only evil continually."

There were Sons of God in the earth, but no daughters; and as these Sons of God only worked evil with the sons and daughters of men, causing every imagination of their hearts to be evil continually, must we not concede the probability of their having been the embodied spirits of Satan and his Angels? A creation by their own Spirit power, permitted from on high, that the inscrutable plans of Heaven might be carried out? We must believe this, and that in this form the serpent appeared before Eve, and talked with her.

The woman said unto the serpent: "We may eat of the fruit of the trees of the garden, but of the fruit of the tree which is in the midst of the garden, God hath said: 'Ye shall not eat of it, neither shall ye touch it, lest ye die.'"

It is not only probable but almost positive, that the only death known by Adam and Eve was that death that the beasts of the field died—the ceasing to exist the blotting out of existence.

They were created from the ground like the others; they lived by the same means of breathing, eating and drinking; they would die the same death. The penalty threatened was not eternal life with eternal torments; but a termination of the entire existence of body and spirit, or soul, if that word be preferred. For "Soul," in the Hebrew, meant the spirit or living principle in the animal body; and was as applicable to beast as to man. Even in the Revelations it is said: "And the second angel poured out his vial upon the sea; and every living soul died in the sea."

The correctness of this view of the penalty is further strengthened by the words of the Lord, immediately after the transgression. In speaking to Adam he said: "In the sweat of thy face shalt thou eat bread, till thou return unto the ground; for out of it wast thou taken; for dust thou art, and unto dust shalt thou return."

And the Lord God said "Behold the man is become as one of us, to know good and evil. And now lest he put forth his hand, and take also of the tree of life and eat, and live forever, therefore the Lord God sent him forth from the Garden of Eden, to till the ground from whence he was taken."

Did this—"and live forever"—have reference to the body or to the spirit? To both the body and the spirit, beyond doubt. For the body had only incurred the penalty of mortality, which penalty would be strictly imposed later on by the dissolution of both body and spirit at the same time; but had they eaten of the tree of life it would, by the law of God governing its virtues, not only have removed the death penalty, but would have secured immortality to them in body and spirit.

It could not have meant the spirit of man, as distinct from his body, and as immortal in its very nature—for the words of the Lord convey most distinctly that the whole man, body and spirit, is nothing but a creature the Lord had made from the ground, and that the tree of life alone could give him immortality either of body or soul.

To judge Adam and Eve by the new dispensation, they committed offence even before they had eaten of the fruit. For the very desire to eat, and in yielding to the desire, the reaching forth of the hand to take it, was wrong; and had they refrained, even then, and not eaten, would they not already have sinned?

And the serpent said unto the woman: "Ye shall not surely die; for God doth know that in the day ye eat thereof, then your eyes shall be opened; and ye shall be as gods, knowing good and evil."

This was a most seductive argument: "To be as gods in the knowledge of good and evil."

"She saw it was good for food, was pleasant to the eyes, and a tree to be desired to make one wise, so she took of the fruit thereof and did eat; and gave also unto her husband with her, and he did eat."

"And the eyes of them both were opened and they knew that they were naked."

When they heard the voice of the Lord God they hid themselves, and on being questioned confessed their guilt, but laid the blame on others. For Adam said: "The woman whom thou gavest to be with me, she gave me of the tree, and I did eat."

And the woman said: "The serpent beguiled me, and I did eat."

We can well believe that Eve thought him some superior being, wise and truthful; and did not know, until her eyes were opened and she knew good and evil, that he was the serpent indeed that had deceived and beguiled her.

The Lord did not question the serpent; he knew him and his every motive; and in the serpent being cursed above all cattle, and above every beast of the field, and in going on his belly and eating dust all his life, the Lord used one as typical of the other. As the one serpent could only crawl in the dust, and in its noiseless, cowardly way, bite at the heel; so would the seed of this great Serpent only bruise the heel of the woman's seed; while hers, in the person of the coming Redeemer, would bruise and crush his head.

Unto the woman he said: "I will greatly multiply the sorrow of thy conception; in sorrow thou shalt bring forth children; and thy desire shall be to thy husband, and he shall rule over thee."

And unto Adam he said: "Cursed is the ground for thy sake; in sorrow shalt thou eat of it all the days of thy life; thorns also and thistles shall it bring forth to thee; and thou shalt eat the herb of the field."

So he drove out the man.

And soon deep trouble overtook them. For their first born, Cain, was, in his heart, the veritable child of Satan, the serpent, and was driven a murderer, a vagabond and a fugitive from the home of his parents and from the face of the Lord. And thus the seed of the serpent, in the person of Cain, began the attack on the seed of the woman, his own mother; and was exiled into the earth, even as his father, the serpent, before him, was cast out from heaven down to the earth.

"And there appeared a great wonder in heaven, a woman clothed with the sun, and the moon under her feet, and upon her head a crown of twelve stars.

"And she being with child cried, travailing in birth, and pained to be delivered."

And there appeared another wonder in heaven, and behold a great red dragon, having seven heads and ten horns, and seven crowns upon his heads.

"And the dragon stood before the woman which was ready to be delivered, for to devour her child as soon as it was born. And she brought forth a man child who was to rule all nations with a rod of iron.

"And the great dragon was cast out of heaven, that old serpent, called the Devil, and Satan, which deceiveth the whole world; he was cast out into the earth. And his angels were cast out with him.

"And when the dragon saw that he was cast unto the earth, he persecuted the woman which brought forth the man child. And to the woman were given two wings of a great eagle, that she might fly into the wilderness, into her place, where she is nourished for a time, and times, and half a time, from the face of the serpent.

"And the serpent cast out of his mouth water as a flood, after the woman, that he might cause her to be carried away of the flood.

"And the earth helped the woman, and the earth opened her mouth and swallowed up the flood which the dragon cast out of his mouth.

"And the dragon was wroth with the woman and went to make war with the remnant of her seed, which kept the commandments of God."

The serpent, in Cain, had destroyed the only son of Adam, but the Lord interposed and drove him forth to his own; and Adam again begat "a son in his own likeness, after his image, and called his name Seth."

And the descendents of Seth called upon the name of the Lord, and walked with him and were blessed.

For they were the seed that would crush the head of the serpent, and the Lord God was with them, and had respect to their offerings, and chose from them such as he had ordained unto eternal life.

Enoch, the son of Jared, walked with God three hundred and sixty-five years, and was not, for God took him.

Noah was a just man, and perfect in his generations; and we have no reason to doubt that during the sixteen hundred and fifty years from the creation of Adam to the coming of the flood, thousands of others were raised up and set apart unto the coming of the new heaven and the new earth.

The children of the promise were keepers of sheep and herders of cattle.

They grazed their flocks and their herds to the south and west of Eden, on the plains of the Euphrates and of the Hiddekel, and roamed through the green forests of the bordering hills.

They walked and mused where God in his creation was ever near; and there, beneath the firmament of heaven, they built their altars of unhewn stone, and sacrificed unto the Lord, and communed with him.

Cain went and dwelt in the land of Nod, east of Eden, and founded a city there. His descendants were expert and cunning in devices.

They used the harp and the organ, and were skilled artificers of brass and iron.

But iniquity and crime followed them all their days, and every evil thing was their portion.

"The earth was full of violence, and it grieved the Lord that he had made man."

Though the descendants of Seth had not forgotten the Lord, yet many were led astray by the Sons of God, and by their wicked kinsmen, the children of Cain.

The Lord would now utterly destroy this mass of reeking crime; would sweep from the earth the hordes of materialized demons who had, for untold ages, polluted it.

He had kept his own, and had saved them whom he would save, despite the serpent and his seed, and he would now destroy man and beast, except the few he willed to preserve in the Ark.

CHAPTER VII.

THE FLOOD AND ITS EXTENT.

Methuselah had just died, aged nine hundred and sixty-nine years. He was two hundred and forty three years old when Adam died, so that these two lives reached from the creation to the flood.

And God looked upon the earth, and behold, it was corrupt; for all flesh had corrupted his way upon the earth. But Noah found grace in the eyes of the Lord.

And God said unto Noah, "The end of all flesh is come before me; for the earth is filled with violence through them; and behold, I will destroy them with the earth. Make thee an Ark of gopher wood, rooms shalt thou make in the Ark, and shalt pitch it within and without with pitch."

"The length of the Ark shall be three hundred cubits (four hundred and seventy-five feet), the breadth of it fifty cubits (seventy-nine feet) and the height of it thirty cubits (forty-seven and a half feet.)"

" A window shalt thou make to the Ark, and a door set in the side; with lower, second and third stories shalt thou make it."

Thus did Noah as the Lord had commanded him.

And the Lord said unto Noah, ''Come thou and all thy house into the Ark; for thee have I seen righteous before me in this generation."

Noah was six hundred years old, and had three sons, Shem, Ham and Japheth, who were near a hundred years of age.

And Noah and his wife, and his three sons and their wives, went into the Ark. And they took in with them fowls of the air, and cattle, and creeping things; in twos of unclean things, and sevens of clean ones. And they took in food for themselves, and for all the creatures that were with them. And they went in as the Lord commanded, and the Lord shut them in.

"And it came to pass, after seven days, that the waters of the flood were upon the earth. And all the fountains of the great deep were broken up, and the windows of heaven were opened."

" And the flood was forty days upon the earth, and the waters prevailed exceedingly, and all the high hills that were under the whole·heaven were covered." .

"Fifteen cubits upward did the waters pre-vail; and the mountains were covered."

And every living substance was destroyed which was upon the face of the ground, both man, and cattle, and creeping things, and the fowl of the heaven; and they were destroyed from the earth, and Noah only remained alive, and they that were with him in the Ark.

'' And the waters prevailed upon the earth a hundred and fifty days."

" And God remembered Noah, and made a wind to pass over the earth, and the waters assuaged; the fountains also of the deep and the windows of heaven were stopped, and the rain from heaven was restrained. And the waters returned from off the earth con-tinually; and after the end of the hundred and fifty days the waters were abated."

And the Ark rested on the mountains of Ararat; and after five and forty days were the tops of the mountains seen.

And in the second month, on the seven and twentieth day, was the earth dried.

And God spake to Noah saying, "Go forth out of the Ark, thou and all that are with thee; and be fruitful and multiply upon the earth.

And Noah builded an altar unto the Lord, and offered burnt offerings on the altar.

And the Lord smelled a sweet savor. ·

"And the Lord said in his heart, 'I will not again curse the ground any more for man's sake: for the imagination of man's heart is evil from his youth; neither will I again smite any more every living thing as I have done. While the earth remaineth, seed time and harvest, and cold and heat, and summer and winter, and day and night, shall not cease."

"And God blessed Noah and his sons, and said unto them, 'Be fruitful and multiply and replenish the earth.'"

" And the fear of you and the dread of you shall be upon every beast of the earth, and upon every fowl of the air, upon all that moveth upon the earth, and upon all the fishes of the sea; into your hand are they delivered."

" Every moving thing that liveth shall be meat for you; even as the green herbs have I given you all things."

" But flesh with the life thereof, which is the blood thereof, shall ye not eat."

" And surely your blood of your lives will I require; at the hand of every beast will I require it; and at the hand of man; at the hand of every man's brother will I require the life of man."

" Whoso sheddeth man's blood, by man shall his blood be shed; for in the image of God made he man."

" And the Lord did set his bow in the cloud, as a token of this everlasting covenant between him and every living thing, that the waters should no more become a flood to destroy all flesh."

The earth was purified with the flood of waters.

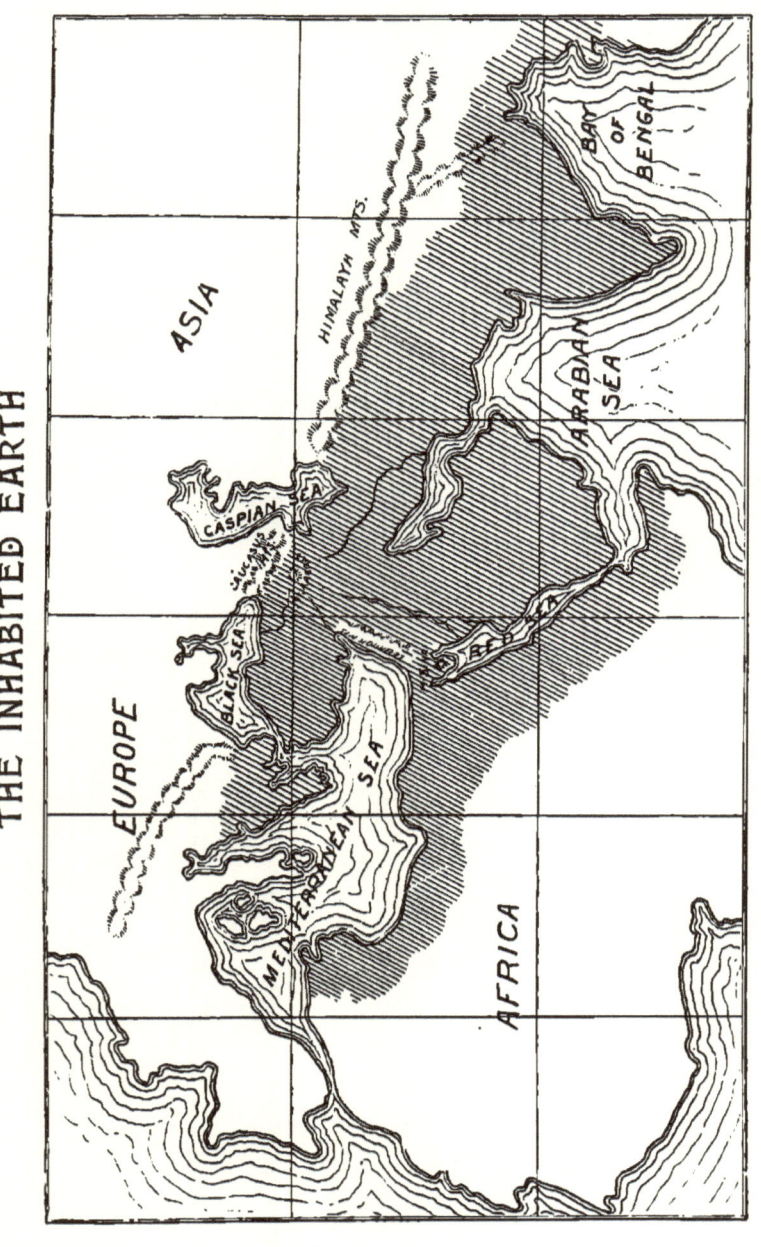

THE INHABITED EARTH

BEFORE THE FLOOD.

ASIA

EUROPE

AFRICA

CASPIAN SEA

BLACK SEA

HIMALAYA MTS.

BAY OF BENGAL

ARABIAN SEA

MEDITERRANEAN SEA

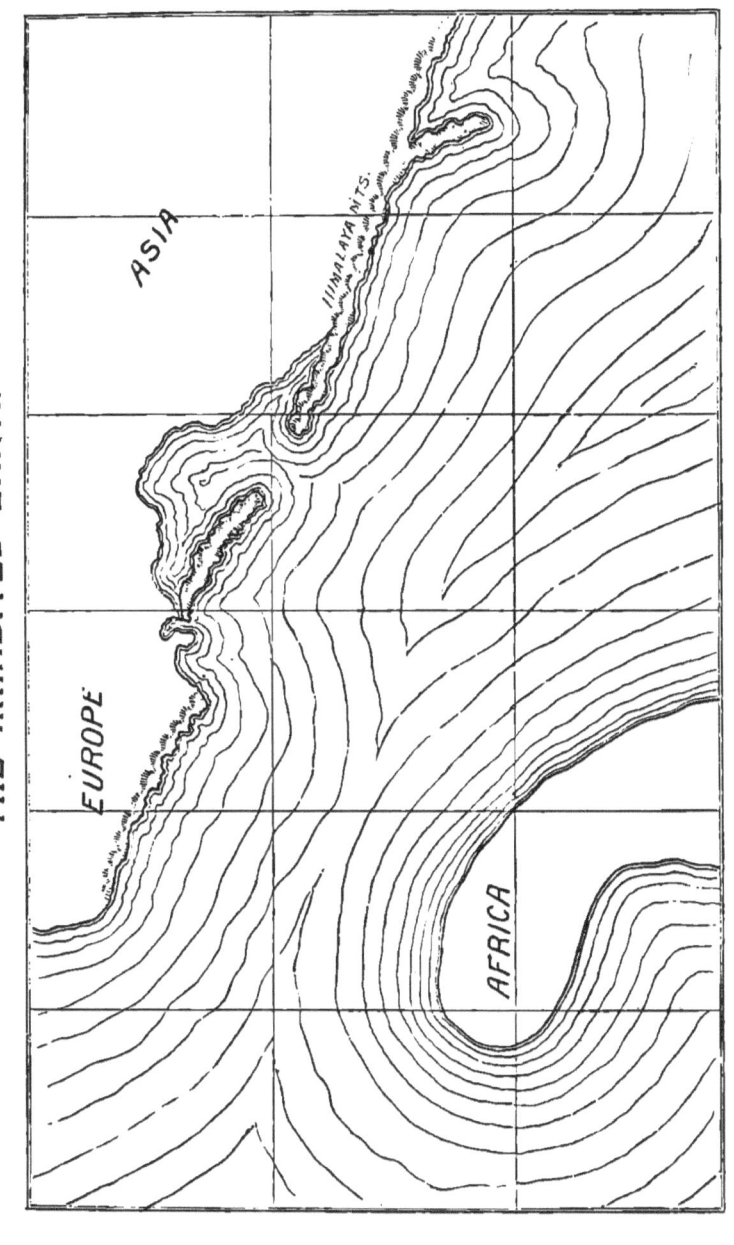

THE INHABITED EARTH DURING THE FLOOD.

Man, and serpents of flesh, and all living creatures with them, were destroyed.

To estimate the number of men that perished would be only wild conjecture. Still it hardly seems probable that there were over three millions drowned.

Although there were some sixteen hundred years in which to multiply and replenish the earth, and the average length of life of those mentioned was near nine hundred years, yet the average age before they begat children was one hundred and ten years, and the ratio of increase, as compared with that of modern times, was very low.

The territory they occupied contained not over four million square miles. And we must also reflect that although probably half of the population were keepers of sheep and cattle; and that their thousands of flocks and herds would require ample grazing room; still their population and their herds did not force the two families of Seth and Cain beyond the distance of visiting neighbors, as is proven by the similarity of their family names.

They had no ancestral names from which

to select and bestow on their children; so we must conclude that this similarity resulted either from consultation between the parents, or because one family knew that the other had already used it.

The following are the names of the eldest or heiring sons, beginning with,

ADAM.

SETH,	CAIN,
ENOS,	ENOCH,
CAINAN,	IRAD,
MAHALALEEL,	MEHUJAEL,
JARED,	METHUSELAH,
ENOCH,	LAMECH,
METHUSELAH,	JABAL,
LAMECH,	
NOAH.	

And furthermore, there is little doubt that they dwelt chiefly along the rich valleys and plateaus of ancient rivers that, heading in the garden of Eden, flowed near the present Euphrates and Tigris; probably stretched somewhat farther eastward toward the Indus, and westward toward the Mediterranean.

But there is no doubt that all the families, all the descendants of Abel, and of Cain, and the iniquitous issue of the sons of God, lived, and sinned, and died in this great basin.

We can now, in part, conceive the magnitude of this catastrophe, and the method of its accomplishment.

The Caucasian mountains on the north, and the Himalayan ranges and spurs on the east, were the walls to hold the waters where men dwelt.

When the time came, and Noah was shut in the Ark, all the land within this enclosure began to sink—to sink lower, lower—and the flood gates of heaven were opened, and it rained day and night.

And while rivers of waters came rushing down the mountain sides, the land was still sinking, slowly sinking, until the fountains of the great deep were broken up.

And the Caspian sea burst forth and rushed southward along the western base of the Himalayas; and the Black and Mediterranean, mingling their angry waters, swept eastward and southward. While on the south, the Red sea, and the Arabian, and the Bay of Bengal, gave way, and the Indian ocean came pouring in; and the waves of waters rolled over and crushed fair cities of frantic men, over plains of fleeing and bellowing cattle and screaming beasts; over Pison and Gihon, over Hiddekel and the Euphrates—on, and on, till all the waters met in great mountain waves, and beat against Himalayas' granite walls.

Mount Horeb slowly sank beneath the waters, and Mount Sinai, and cedar covered Lebanon, and craggy Ararat.

Fifteen cubits upward did the waters prevail—all the mountains were covered; all the known world was beneath the flood.

And the waters prevailed upon the earth a hundred and fifty days.

But God remembered Noah, and made a wind to pass over the earth, and the waters assuaged. The fountains also of the deep, and the windows of heaven were stopped.

And the earth slowing rising, the waters returned from off the earth continually, and after the end of the hundred and fifty days the waters were abated, and the Ark rested on the mountains of Ararat; and after five and forty days were the tops of the mountains seen rising from the waters.

And in the second month, on the seventh and twentieth day, was the earth dried.

CHAPTER VIII.

FROM THE FLOOD TO MOSES.

"And Noah and his sons, and all living things that were with them in the Ark, went forth to multiply and replenish the earth."

Mankind was no longer restricted to a diet of fruits and herbs, but was permitted to eat the flesh of all kinds of animals, fish and fowls. But one condition was imposed, one clear, emphatic command given, that is equally binding on all mankind at this day, and that was, that they should not eat the "life of the flesh which is the blood thereof."

And immediately thereafter the life of man began to shorten. Noah's reached the usual length—nine hundred and fifty years, but Shem's only six hundred.

Three hundred years after the flood the life of man had decreased to less than two hundred.

Abram died, aged one hundred and

seventy-five; Jacob, one hundred and forty-seven; and it is quite probable that the average life of mankind at that time did not exceed three score years and ten.

Shem, Ham and Japhet begat sons and daughters; and marriages occurring now at an early age, and there being no wars or plagues to destroy, the increase was rapid. In the days of Peleg, who was born one hundred years after the flood, men must have become very numerous; for having, in their migrations, reached the plain of Shinar, they there began to build the tower of Babel. But the Lord seeing evil in their design, confounded their language, and scattered them from thence over the face of the earth; and at that time was the earth divided.

Three hundred and fifty-two years after the flood there was born in Ur of the Chaldees, Abram, the son of Terah, a man whom the Lord promised to bless above all men, whose seed should be as the sand on the sea shore and as the stars in heaven for number, of whom should be a nation and company of nations, and kings should come out of his loins; and in his seed should all the nations of the earth be blessed.

When Abram was seventy-five years old the Lord commanded him to leave Haran, and to go and behold the country he would show him.   So he took his wife, Sarah, who was also his half sister, and his nephew, Lot, and all their substance, and went southward through Canaan, the promised land.

They wandered to and fro through the country, and at the end of ten years were settled; Abram in Mamre, and Lot in or near Sodom.

It was while living there that Abram, after the slaughter of Chedorlaomer and of the kings that were with him, came to Salem and paid tribute to Melchizedek, the king thereof, and who was also a priest of the most high God.

It is probable that Melchizedek was Shem; for Shem lived for sixty-five years after that, and Noah had died eighty-seven years before.

Abram lived in the vale of Mamre for many years, and while living there the cities

of Sodom and Gomorrah became so fearfully
wicked that the Lord sent two angels and
destroyed them, and all the people of the
plain, by raining on them fire and brimstone.

When Abram got up early the morning
they were destroyed, and looked toward the
two cities, behold the smoke of the country
went up as the smoke of a furnace.

It seems probable that previous to the
destruction of these cities and the plain, the
river Jordan ran entirely through Arabia, and
emptied into the Red sea.

There are indications of some large river
having at one time ran through western
Arabia, ran from the north, and had along its
banks a nation or nations of people, greatly
skilled in architecture, as is evidenced by
some splendid ruins remaining to this day.

But the Jordan now empties its clear
waters into that great cess-pool, the Dead
sea, and nearly all south of there is given
over to desolation.

We can not but wonder at the minute
description of the appearance and the peculiar acts of the three angels that came to

destroy these cities of the plain of Siddim.

"Abram sat in the tent door in the heat of the day.

"And he lifted up his eyes and looked, and lo! three men stood by him, and when he saw he ran to met them from the tent door and bowed himself toward the ground.

"And said; 'My Lord, if now I have found favor in thy sight pass not away, I pray thee, from thy servant. Let a little water, I pray thee, be fetched and wash your feet, and rest yourselves under the tree.

"And I will fetch a morsel of bread and comfort ye your hearts; after that ye shall pass on; for therefore are ye come to your servant." And they said, "So do, as thou hast said." And Abraham hastened into the tent unto Sarah, and said, "Make ready quickly three measures of fine meal, knead it and make cakes upon the hearth." And Abraham ran unto the herd and fetched a calf tender and good and gave it unto a young man; and he hastened to dress it."

"And he took butter and milk, and the calf which he had dressed and set it before them; and he stood by them under the tree and *they did eat.*"

" And there came two angels to Sodom at even, and Lot seeing them rose up to meet them, and he bowed himself with his face toward the ground.

" And he said, ' Behold now my Lord turn in, I pray you, into your servant's house and tarry all night, and wash your feet and ye shall rise up early and go on your ways."

"And he pressed upon them greatly, and they turned in unto him and entered into his house, and he made them a feast and did bake unleavened bread and *they did eat.*

After the feast when Lot was expostulating with the Sodomites, the men put forth their hands and pulled Lot into the house to them and shut the door.

And when the morn arose and while he lingered, the men laid hold upon his hand and upon the hand of his wife, and upon the hand of his two daughters, and they brought him forth and set him without the city.

These angels of the Lord had all the

physical, material properties of men. They talked as men face to face with Abraham and Sarah, and with Lot and his family; they ate with Abraham and partook of the feast with Lot. And they put forth their hands and pulled Lot into the house with the physical touch and force of man. And likewise the next morning they took Lot and his family by the hand and led them forth from Sodom.

And Jacob, when in or near the country of Edom, wrestled with a man until the break of day, and when the man saw that he prevailed not, he touched Jacob in the hollow of the thigh and lamed him. And this was an angel of the Lord.

Can we not then conclude with reason that Satan and his angels could also take unto themselves physical bodies, when necessary to accomplish their evil purposes?

Abraham, for the hundred years that he lived after leaving Haran, had no permanent abiding place, but was a wanderer in the land promised to his seed.

He died and was succeeded by his son Isaac. He also, like his father, Abraham, pitched his tent and grazed his flocks wherever seemed to him best.

And he in turn was succeeded by his son Jacob, the twin brother of Esau. Esau was the elder, but was perverse, and married Canaanitish women; and being by his mother's partiality for Jacob, and by her cunning, deprived of his father's blessing, he threatened to kill his brother. So Jacob fled to Haran where his relations lived; and there he married two of his cousins, Rachel and Leah, and from these two, and their two hand maids or servants, sprung the twelve tribes of Israel.

The cup of iniquity of the inhabitants of Canaan was not yet full, and Israel and his children, his sons and his grand sons, numbered but seventy souls.

So driven out of Canaan by reason of the drought there, Jacob went into Egypt unto his son Joseph whom the Lord had sent before to prepare the way for him, and finding favor with Pharaoh, the king of the country, he and his family and their herds were placed in the land of Goshen, the most de-

sirable part of the kingdom. And there
they remained for over two hundred years
protected and nourished by the most powerful people of those times; increased and
grew into a nation of themselves, a nation
great and wealthy.

But the time was drawing nigh for them
to return and occupy the land promised to
Abraham, to Isaac and to Jacob.

The Egyptians were becoming jealous of
their great wealth and growth as a distinct
people, and were hard taskmasters unto them.

But oppression and tyranny would make
them the more willing to obey the command
of the Lord, to go forth on their long journey to the land of Canaan.

And Pharaoh's heart would be hardened
that he would object to their going, and the
Lord would do wonderful things, and would
take out his people with an uplifted arm.

CHAPTER IX.

EXODUS OF THE JEWS FROM EGYPT.

The Bible makes no allusion to any form of idolatry having prevailed before the flood, and perhaps there was none. Satan and his angels, in the sons of God and their off-spring, were ever present; so that images and incantations were hardly possible, and not at all probable. Imbued with the spirit of Satan himself, and probably fully cognizant of it, they had nothing of superior evil to fear.

But the flood came and destroyed all flesh, and it may have been that these spirits of evil that could only be drowned as to their bodies of flesh, as the swine were drowned in the Sea of Galilee, were re-strained from ever again dwelling on earth as before the flood, and could only enter into and occupy those human bodies already created.

They found a speedy lodgement in the

person of Ham, whom they influenced to do evil; and, as generation after generation came and passed away, their power grew, until they controlled all mankind. Families, and people, and nations, had their gods of gold, and silver, and stone; their Baal, their Ashtoreth, their Chemosh, their Molech, at whose shrines they offerred sacrifices, and bowed down and worshipped.

The descendants of Shem were idolaters, and servants of Satan, as was the whole world, with a few exceptions of individuals whom the Lord had chosen and sealed for himself.

When Jacob moved from Padanaram his best loved wife, Rachael, stole her father's images, and probably had them with her when she died.

That the Israelites were idolaters while they sojourned in Egypt is proven by their making the golden calf, even while the cloud of the Lord was on the mountain above them. And after their settlement in Canaan, by their continuous lapsing into sacrificing unto the various idols of that country.

No branch of the human family was more utterly depraved, more corrupt and given over to the working of every iniquity, than were those descendants of Ham, the Canaanites. The destruction of Sodom and Gomorrah by fire from heaven, in the days of Abraham, was a special and unprecedented punishment for enormity of crime.

The Egyptians were also descendants of Ham, and with their idols had a system of priests, magicians and sorcerers, whom the Lord would now confound and punish.

The Israelites were not a people that were especially better than others.

They did not choose the Lord as their king and law giver, but the Lord chose them, as he had promised Abraham, and in accordance with his own designs and plans from the beginning.

They were always a rebellious and stiff necked people, whom the most severe and oft repeated punishments could not make obedient.

But the Lord knew from the first what they would do, and, having accomplished

those things for which they were chosen, he
drove them forth from his presence, and scattered them to the four corners of the earth,
never again to be his people, but as long as
time would last to be a reproach and a by-
word amongst all nations.

It seems probable that the Lord did not
make himself known to the Hebrews during
their entire sojourn in Egypt.   For when he
appeared to Moses in a burning bush, at the
foot of Mt. Horeb, he said unto Moses; " I
have surely seen the affliction of my people
which are in Egypt, and have heard their cry
by reason of their task masters; for I know
their sorrows, and I am come down to deliver
them out of the hands of the Egyptians.
Come now, therefore, and I will send thee unto Pharaoh, that thou mayest bring forth my
people, the children of Israel, out of Egypt."

" And Moses said unto God, ' Behold
when I come unto the children of Israel, and
shall say unto them, the God of your fathers
hath sent me unto you; and they shall say to
me, ' What is his name?'   What shall I say
unto them ?"

This was a strange question for Moses to ask, and shows clearly that he, as well as the other Israelites, had little, if any, knowledge of the God of their fathers, of Abraham, Isaac and Jacob.

So Moses returned from Midian unto Egypt, taking with him the rod which at Mt. Horeb had become a serpent, and taking also with him his brother Aaron, who had gone into the wilderness to meet him, and who would continue with him as spokesman, and went into the presence of Pharaoh to perform those wonders that would show the Egyptians, and the Israelites, that there was no one in all the earth like the Lord.

For this very purpose had the Lord raised up Pharaoh, and hardened his heart and the heart of his people, that he might multiply his signs and his wonders in the land of Egypt. And in the nature and sequence of these wonders there is something strangely symbolic. To place them in the order of their occurrence they stand thus:

Are we not justified in thinking that these are typical of man's life from the garden of Eden to the end of time?

THE SERPENTS—Symbolize the fall of man, and also that the Lord would finally be victorious, even as the serpent of his creation did overcome and devour those of the magicians.

THE BLOOD—That shed by Cain when he killed Abel, the first fruits of the fall, and indicative of the violence and crime that would follow.

THE FROGS, LICE AND FLIES—The inflictions that no doubt were visited on men in the days of Adam and Methuselah.

THE MURRAIN—The flood that destroyed all life where men dwelt.

BOILS, HAIL, LOCUSTS—The visitations of divine wrath that man often suffered after the flood.

THE DARKNESS (for three days)—The time that the Savior would remain in the tomb, and probably also emblematical of the great blindness that would always prevail even after the Sun of Righteousness had risen.

For as the hearts of the Egyptians were hardened, and their eyes blinded, so would it be with the Israelites at last; and with other nations and people.

DEATH—The slaying of the first born throughout all of Egypt, as Cain, the first born of Satan, slew Abel, the first born of

Adam; and also pointing to the final termination and blotting out of all earthly things.

"About midnight will I go out into the midst of Egypt."

"And all the first born in the land of Egypt shall die; from the first born of Pharaoh that setteth upon his throne, even unto the first born of the maid servant that is behind the mill; and all the first born of beasts. And there shall be a great cry throughout all the land of Egypt, such as there was none like it, nor shall be like it any more."

How seldom, after the fall, was the first born of men ever chosen of the Lord.

To the second, or some younger son, was nearly always accorded supremacy. Abel, Shem, Abram, Isaac, Jacob, Judah and Moses were eminent examples of this mystic decree of heaven.

But the time came when even as the first born of Eve was the child of Satan, the prince of darkness, so the first born of another woman, Mary, was the son, the only begotten son, of the King of Heaven.

So the Lord did wondrous things before Pharaoh and his servants, destroyed them with plagues, and brought judgments on their gods, the gods whose priests were servants of Satan, and in his name did miracles for a time.

Having finished all his terrible judgments, and crushed the Egyptians into the dust, he brought forth his people Israel, with an outstretched arm.

For he had said unto the children of Israel: "I am the Lord, and I will bring you out from under the burdens of the Egyptians, and I will rid you of their bondage, and I will redeem you with a stretched-out arm, and with great judgments.

"And I will take you for a people, and I will be to you a God; and ye shall know that I am the Lord, your God, which bringeth you out from under the burdens of the Egyptians."

And nothing but Omnipotent power could

have accomplished this great work. The mind is bewildered at its magnitude.

As there were about six hundred thousand men over twenty years old and fit to go forth to war, the entire people must therefore have numbered at least four million of human souls, besides their herds and flocks.

All this vast army of helpless beings were to be taken across the desert in Egypt, across the Red Sea, and the great desert of Arabia; to be fed, and led, and protected like little children.

Nothing is more wonderful, more awe-inspiring in all Biblical history, than these forty years of pilgrimage of the house of Israel.

From the very instant of their leaving the land of Goshen, the Lord had sent his angel to guide them in a pillar of cloud by day, and of fire by night. And when at the end of their third day's journey they had reached the Red sea, and Pharaoh and his great army had overtaken them—for the Lord had again hardened Pharaoh's heart, and induced him to follow with all his chariots and his army, and he pursued and drew nigh unto them— then the pillar of a cloud removed back and rested between the two armies, and unto the Egyptians it was a cloud and darkness, but to the camp of Israel it gave light by night.

"And Moses stretched out his hand over the sea, and the Lord caused the sea to go back by a strong east wind all that night, and made the sea a dry land, and the waters were divided."

"And the children of Israel went into the midst of the sea upon the dry ground, and the waters were a wall unto them on their right hand and on their left."

The Red Sea was about fifteen miles wide where they crossed, and from five to twenty-five feet deep. The roadway must have been some two hundred feet wide to have enabled them to cross over in one night.

And all that long night, while the Egyptians rested and slept in the darkness of one side of the cloud, the other side threw its bright light straight along that marvelous road to the farther shore—and hurrying, pouring steadily on between the crystal walls, were the fleeing hosts of Israel. All the long night the heavenly brightness glowed, the walls of waters stood firm and immovable as the everlasting hills, until the last of Israel had safely reached the shore. But in the early morn, while they were yet crossing, the cloud of darkness was removed from before the eyes of Pharaoh and his army, and, seeing the Israelites fleeing, they rushed thither along the same road. The Lord delayed them by taking off their chariot wheels, but they still pursued, until all were in the waters, Pharaoh and his six hundred chariots, and his captains, and his great army; and then the walls of waters were loosed, and rushed together with a great noise, and overthrew and drowned all the Egyptians, so that not one of them escaped with his life. Truly the Lord of Hosts had brought forth his people with signs and wonders, and with a stretched-out arm, and had executed judgment on the gods of Egypt.

And now safe from further pursuit, and guided by the angel of the Lord, they commenced their journey across the sandy desert, towards the promised land.

And when their provisions gave out the Lord rained them bread from heaven. It fell at night with the dew, and in the morning when the dew was dried the manna was found on the ground. It was white like frost and fine as coriander seed—and when ground in a mortar and baked, it tasted like wafers made with honey. The people gathered enough for one day's use only—if they gathered more it bred worms and stank. On Saturdays two days' portion fell and was gathered, as none fell on Sunday. And this extra portion did not spoil as on other days.

And this bread, provided by the angel of God, never failed in all the forty years that the millions of Israel roamed the dreary wastes of Arabia.

And when they became thirsty, if they found water that was bitter the angel made it sweet and wholesome; if they found none, he would bring a gushing fountain from the solid rock.

And so they journeyed on, following the cloud of God until they reached Mt. Sinai, and there they camped. And Moses went up unto God, and the Lord called unto him out of the mountain saying: "Tell the children of Israel; ye have seen what I did unto the Egyptians, and how I bear you on eagle wings and brought you unto myself."

"Now, therefore, if you will obey my voice indeed, and keep my covenant, then ye shall be a peculiar treasure unto me above all people; for all the earth is mine. And ye shall be unto me a kingdom of priests and a holy nation."

And when Moses told the people as the Lord had commanded him, all the people answered and said; "All that the Lord hath spoken we will do."

And the Lord said unto Moses: "Lo, I come unto thee in a thick cloud, that the people may hear when I speak with thee, and believe thee forever."

And the Lord said unto Moses: "Go

unto the people and sanctify them to-day and
to-morrow, and let them wash their clothes,
and be ready against the third day; for
the third day the Lord will come down in
the sight of all the people upon Mount
Sinai."

And it came to pass on the third day, in
the morning, that there were thunders and
lightnings, and a thick cloud upon the mount,
and the voice of the trumpet exceeding loud;
so that all the people that was in the camp
trembled.

And Moses brought forth the people out
of the camp to meet with God; and they
stood at the nether part of the mount.

And Mount Sinai was altogether on a
smoke, because the Lord descended upon it
in fire; and the smoke thereof ascended as
the smoke of a furnace, and the whole mount
quaked greatly. And when the voice of the
trumpet sounded long, and waxed louder and
louder, Moses spake and God answered him
by a voice. And all the people saw the
thunderings, and the lightnings, and the
noise of the trumpet, and the mountain

smoking, and they removed and stood afar off.   And they said unto Moses: "Speak thou with us, and we will hear; but let not God speak with us, lest we die."

And Moses said unto them: "Fear not, for God is come to prove you; and that his fear may be before your faces, that ye sin not."

And the people stood afar off, and Moses drew near unto the thick darkness where God was.

And the Lord said unto Moses: "Thus shalt thou say unto the children of Israel: Ye have seen that I have talked with you from heaven.

"Ye shall not make with me gods of silver, neither shall ye make unto you gods of gold.

"An altar of earth thou shalt make unto me, and shall sacrifice thereon thy burnt offerings, and thy peace offerings, thy sheep and thine oxen; in all places where I record my name I will come unto thee, and I will bless thee."

And there, midst thunderings and lightnings, with the people standing afar off, he gave unto them his commandments and his ordinance, which they were to observe and obey through all their generations.

These were the first and only code of divine laws ever issued, and upon them are founded all civil law and equity.

CHAPTER X.

THE JEWS IN THE WILDERNESS AND IN CANAAN.

And the Lord there gave unto them laws to govern their every relation of life, as families, as fellow citizens, as subjects of the great King of heaven. No contingencies that could arise were left unprovided for; no obligations or requirements undetermined.

And Moses provided two stones, and the Lord wrote thereon the laws of the covenant, that they could be preserved; and directed Moses to build an ark in which to keep the stones, and above the ark a mercy seat where the Lord would appear unto his priests, and which should be a holy place; and a tabernacle, to enclose these sacred things.

The most minute directions were given for the construction of all these, and workmen were especially endowed with wisdom and cunning for the purpose.

Every detail of official duty and ceremony

was clearly prescribed; and even the tribe, and individuals of the tribe, selected to minister and serve in the house of God.

He had indeed taken this great nation of Israelites as his own chosen people, and had blessed them beyond all the families of the earth, and had shown them signs, and wonders, and great judgments; the like of which the world never saw before, and never would again.

And he would continue to be their God and the source of every earthly blessing to them; would go before and weaken the hearts of their enemies; would tear down the walled cities and send plagues on the inhabitants thereof.

He would make these children of Abraham a nation of priests, a people holy unto himself, if they would only obey his commands and observe his statutes to do them.

But they rebelled even while the glory of the Lord covered the mountain before them. Although they had seen his fierce anger against the Egyptians, and his loving kindness toward themselves; that he had brought them thus far safely, and was even then feeding them with bread from heaven; yet they rebelled, denied his authority over them, and had Aaron make for them an idol of gold, before which they bowed down and worshipped.

Does it seem possible for human intelligence to have been so obtuse? Or must we conclude that they were purposely blinded, and given over to Satan?

A few thousands were slain, and the rest repented.

Ten different times did they incur the anger of God; as many times as there had been plagues sent against Egypt. Still he did not destroy them, but punished and forgave.

For he remembered his covenant with Abraham, Isaac and Jacob, to give Canaan unto their seed for an inheritance; and he would give it them. But all those who were twenty years old and upward when they came out of Egypt, six hundred thousand men, fit for war, none of these, except Caleb and Joshua, should ever enter into the promised land.

They had no doubt been idolaters in Egypt, and were not fit to be servants of the only true God. So they were kept wandering in the wilderness for forty years, until all had died and their bodies been buried in the sands of the desert.

There had grown up now unto Israel an army of six hundred thousand fighting men who had never bowed the knee to idols. They had been in the continuous presence and service of the Lord for forty years; had seen all of his wonders, his infinite power, and his never-failing care of them; had learned to reverence and obey; and would now be taken into Canaan, a land that flowed with milk and honey, and which would be unto them an everlasting inheritance, if they continued obedient unto God.

Entering Canaan with this great army, and assisted by the Lord, they attacked the cities and destroyed all the people; all the men, women and children; and all wherein was the breath of life; tore down the altars of their gods, cut down their groves, and burned their graven images. For the sins of these people of Canaan were great, the cup of their iniquity was full; and the Lord would utterly destroy them from the face of the earth.

So the Lord established his people in this garden spot of all the earth, allotted them their separate possessions, and placed the fear of them and the dread of them on all the neighboring nations.

They had nothing to fear, for the Lord was with them to guide and bless; nothing to fear but the sure and fearful punishment that would be visited on them, should they serve other gods as did the Canaanites before them. And well they knew this, for it was given them as the first and most emphasized of the ten commandments.

And God spake these words saying: "I am the Lord God which have brought thee out of the land of Egypt, out of the house of bondage."

"Thou shalt have no other gods before me."

"Thou shalt not make unto thee any graven image, or any likeness of anything that is in heaven above, or that is in the earth beneath, or that is in the water under the earth."

" Thou shalt not bow down thyself to them, nor serve them, for I, the Lord thy God, am a jealous God, visiting the iniquity of the fathers upon the children unto the third and fourth generation of them that hate me, and showing mercy unto thousands of them that love me and keep my commandments."

The Lord knew the proneness of men to worship images and similitudes, and though it might be one representative of the Lord himself, it would be none the less an act of idolatry.

Moses said unto the Hebrews: " The day that thou stoodest before the Lord thy God in Horeb, and you came near and stood under the mountain, and the mountain burned with fire unto the midst of heaven, with darkness, clouds and thick darkness:

" And the Lord spake unto you out of the midst of fire; ye heard the voice of the words, but saw no similitude; only ye heard a voice. Take ye therefore good heed unto yourselves (for ye saw no manner of similitude on the day that the Lord spake unto you in Horeb out of the midst of the fire).

" Lest ye corrupt yourselves and make you a graven image the similitude of any figure, the likeness of male or female."

There must be no worship of intermediate things, no bowing down before anything in heaven above or in the earth beneath. The only true, acceptable worship is unto the Lord God himself, for all else is an abomination in his sight.

Moses, before his death, had written out all the laws for his people, had rehearsed all the wonderful things that the Lord had done for them up to that time, enumerated the great blessings that would attend obedience to the laws, and the fearful calamities that would follow disobedience. And, after his death, as Joshua, his successor, lead them forward, when they came to the river Jordan and would cross over, he called to him all the chief men of the congregation to see what the Lord would do for him, even as he had done for Moses. So when the bearers of the ark stepped in the edge of the waters, the river, although at a flood and overrunning its banks, stopped flowing and stood up on either hand, until all the people had passed over, and the ark also had reached dry land.

And afterwards, when fighting the five Kings of the Armorites before Gibeon, Joshua said, in the sight of Israel, "Sun, stand thou still upon Gibeon, and thou, moon, in the valley of Ajalon."

And the sun stood still and the moon stayed until the people avenged themselves upon their enemies. So the sun stood still in the midst of heaven, and hasted not to go down about a whole day.

And there was no day like that before it or after it, that the Lord hearkened unto the voice of a man; for the Lord fought for Israel.

During all the life of Joshua there was war continually in subduing and destroying the inhabitants of the country, as the Lord had commanded them.

And the Lord was with them in their

battles, sending down great hail from heaven to kill the Canaanites, and armies of hornets to drive them from the country.

And after Joshua died the wars continued, for the country was not yet all subdued, neither had all the children of Israel secured their inheritance. And even after all of the tribes had become settled in their possessions, and were free to enjoy the fruits of their labors, peace and plenty were never theirs for more than a few years at a time.

"For after the death of Joshua and of the elders that outlived him, there arose another generation after them which knew not the Lord, nor yet the works which he had done for Israel.

"And the children of Israel did evil in the sight of the Lord and served Baalim.

"And when the Lord raised them up judges, then the Lord was with the judge, and delivered them out of the hand of their enemies all the days of the judge (for it repented the Lord because of their groanings by reason of them that oppressed them and vexed them). And it came to pass when the judge was dead, that they returned and corrupted themselves more than their fathers in following other gods to serve them ; they ceased not from their own doings nor from their stubborn way."

The history of the Jewish nation for the fifteen hundred years of its existence, from the exodus from Egypt until its final dispersion, was but a repetition of these four incidents : idolatry, punishment, repentance, forgive-ness.

The Lord was there with the ark of the covenant, and was carrying out his own plans.

He had his thousands and tens of thous-ands of true followers, whom the devil could not seduce to idolatry.

He had great and wise kings who served him ; he had legions of prophets who warned the wicked and comforted the right-eous, and revealed the hidden things of God.

David, the chosen of the Lord, the great warrior, the grand psalmist, reigned four hundred years after the Israelites entered

Canaan ; Solomon, his son, and the wisest and richest of kings, built the temple of the Lord, and the Jewish nation was at the zenith of its power and glory.

Four hundred years more and the temple was destroyed, the ark of the covenant disappeared, never to be found again, and the children of Israel were led into captivity.

They returned some fifty years after, but were never the same again. The fear of them and the dread of them no longer existed among the nations. Their idolatries were nearly national, and they were speedily lapsing into all the iniquities of the Gentiles. Still the Lord did not forget his covenant with Abraham, Isaac and Jacob. He was always with their seed to bless or to punish. He held them together as a people distinct from all others, a people with his mark upon them that would not be removed as long as the world endured. And they grew still less potential in the world's history. They were a prey to various nations, for while others increased they decreased, and their servitude finally became continuous and grievous.

But a king was promised them, a king of the stock of David, who would redeem and rule his people of Israel. They knew of but one kind of kingly authority, and that was the kind exercised by David, a king who would lead them forth to destroy and subdue, a king and a mighty warrior, who could break the yoke of the Roman bondage.

For fifteen hundred years the house of Israel had been familiar with the mighty works of the Lord.

They were his chosen people, and he was not only their God, but their King, who had unnumbered times directed their wars, planned their battles, and insured them victory. If he now would send them a king they would expect one, as of old, vested with earthly power and clothed in regal splendor. Miracles were still being performed, probably more than the stirring of the waters of the pool of Siloam; so that the healing of the sick, or causing the blind to see, was not a convincing attestation of divine authority to this people to whom the Lord was wont to appear with signs, and wonders, and manifestations of Almighty power.

A king was promised, a king was looked for, and none but the one coming vested with kingly attributes would be accepted by this wilful, stiff-necked people.

The centuries had rolled by, and all the covenants of the Lord had been kept. Unto the seed of Abraham had been the promises, and they had attained unto all, except that which then drew nigh to fulfillment. But they did not comprehend it, neither do they unto this day. For their hearts were hardened, and their eyes were blinded that they could not see.

The Lord had always manifested himself to man as Jehovah — the Almighty Creator and Ruler of the universe—had rained fire and brimstone on the wicked, had sent fearful plagues on great nations of idolaters, had talked to man midst thunderings and lightnings and quaking mountains. But now a new dispensation would begin, one affecting the heart of man; quiet, subdued, spiritual, as was symbolized by the still small voice with which the Lord on

Mt. Horeb manifested himself unto Moses.

And the new dynasty would have but one king, Emanuel, the Prince of Peace; and he would not reign on earth, neither would he remove the political bondage; but he would save his people, Gentile as well as Jew, from the bondage of sin, and, in a new heaven and a new earth, would reign as King and sovereign Lord for ever and ever.

CHAPTER XI.

THE DESIGNS OF OMNIPOTENCE, UNALTERABLE AND MERCIFUL.

Before proceeding further, we will return to the farthest past of man's existence, and, making a general resume of the most important events, endeavor to make such conclusions as events seem to warrant.

No one who believes in an Omnipotent Creator can, for an instant, doubt that when He created Adam and Eve he had designs and plans that extended through all time for their completion.

That these plans could not possibly be frustrated, nor in the least interfered with, is also beyond question.

The very quality of infinity is of such absoluteness as precludes the possibility of effective resistance or interference.

We must accept in the fullest sense of infinity every attribute of the God of the

universe, and rest always in the perfect assurance that nothing ever has occurred, or
ever can occur, in opposition to his will.

We must, therefore, conclude with certainty that his plans were exactly carried
out. Why were two created, a male and a
female, and commanded to multiply and replenish the earth, if there had been even a
possibility of their always remaining in the
garden of Eden ?

And the placing of the forbidden tree in
such convenient and conspicuous proximity,
its subtle temptation, aided and made sure
by the chief spirit of all evil, resulted only
in accordance with the divine plan—that
plan which, conceived millions of years before, had gradually, through the unnumbered
ages, progressed and unfolded to the point
where the great Red Dragon would renew
his warfare against the king of heaven.

But there would be this difference in the
contest : Then it was amidst and against the
realms of his rightful sovereign; now it would
be carried on in his own ancient kingdom,
and his defeat would be final and eternal.

We have no reason to think that Satan was cognizant of the plans of the Lord. But the Lord had said : "Let us make man in our image, after our likeness." And having made him, and placed him in a carefully prepared garden, with the fruit of the trees of life and death before him, Satan entered there, and with him death.

And after Satan, in his son Cain, had killed Abel, the son of Adam, the Lord restrained him, and drove him hence.

And another son having been born unto Adam, the Lord began raising unto himself those spirits of immortality that would eventually reoccupy the forfeited kingdom of Satan and his angels.

And the method of obstruction adopted by Satan—the tempting of Adam to mortality—was made thus to recoil on his own followers.

For the wicked, in dying, would die to all eternity; while the chosen of the Lord would die indeed, as all must die, but, by a plan that would be consummated four thousand years after, they would, at the last, be raised up from death and the grave, to life and immortality.

And this plan of redemption from death would revert back and cover all the elect from the very beginning of time ; and that, too, without any knowledge on their part of any of the circumstances, conditions or provisions of this plan.

They were the spirits that the Lord had created for himself, were obedient to his commands, and would be redeemed from death.

While those not chosen and elected for eternal life would simply be left inheritors of eternal oblivion.

Why should we think otherwise ? Consider, for a moment, the incidents of the transgression of Adam. He had just been created ; was utterly ignorant of all spiritual existence ; was simple and trusting. The angel of the Lord told him not to eat of the fruit of a certain tree, for if he did, he would die; and the angel left him. Another angel soon appeared, an evil angel, and told him that he would not die if he ate of the fruit, but, on the contrary, would become wise as a god, knowing good and evil. He ate without hesitation, and became mortal, just as he would have become immortal had he eaten of the tree of life.

But nearly all men believe that man was created immortal. If he was immortal, eating of the forbidden fruit could not have made him mortal. So they say that this penalty of death was applicable to the immortal spirit in man, and meant in reality its eternal punishment, its never-ending torments in the flames and amidst the fiery serpents of the deepest hell prepared for the devil and his angels, and where the flames of the burning, and the cries and groans of agony, would never cease, day nor night, through all eternity.

Is it possible that the majority of men have such a poor conception of the infinite mercy, the infinite justice, of the God of the universe?

If Adam was immortal and perfect, what was the object of the temptation? Could it possibly add in any way whatever to the happiness of man, or to the glory of God?

And suppose that he had withstood the temptation, what then?

As he did not stand, but fell, what was gained?

Do they think that the Lord was experimenting with his new creation; and as he had not made him strong enough to withstand the temptation, he would therefore cast the majority, the vast majority, of his descendents into the everlasting torments of hell?

Man, proud, vain, boastful man, considers and esteems himself as too important a factor in the universe; he conceives that for him, as the lord of all the earth, was the sun made to give light by day, and the moon and the stars light by night; and that he, in the power of his mind and in the brightness and keenness of his intellect, is but little inferior to the angels of God.

He can not reconcile himself to the truth, that he is but dust of the earth; but grass that is cut down and withered; a lighted taper that is blown out, and is gone.

Possessed of this feeling of vain importance he would rather consign ninety-nine one hundredths of the entire human race to eternal torments, than to consent to oblivion for the unredeemed, and thereby justify the mercy and loving kindness of his God.

Does he ever reflect on the almost total ignorance of all religious obligations that has always existed amongst men? And the entire absence of consideration for the lives of men, when the Lord has visited them in his wrath?

There were no preachers of righteousness, before the flood; no warnings to the wicked of eternal sufferings hereafter.

But the flood came, and all were drowned in their sins. Of the millions on earth only eight were saved alive.

After the flood all men fell immediately into idolatry, and all forms of iniquity that were abhorent to the Lord.

Even the descendents of Noah who, it is supposed, founded the Chinese empire, are the most obdurate of idolaters unto this day. Abram was called from amidst the idols of his people and given a mission and ordained to a destiny by the Lord to accomplish his own designs.

There was a Melchisedek, a priest of the most high God; but, so far as we are informed, all that surrounded him were servants of Satan.

Sodom and Gomorrah were pre-eminently corrupt; to such degree that the Lord sent an angel to destroy them; but he sent none to warn.

When the Israelites were about to leave Egypt for the land of Canaan, the hearts of the Egyptians were hardened by the Lord that he might show his signs and his great wonders.

And he not only afflicted them in their bodies and in their property, but in the last plague sent he killed all of their first born, not only of beasts, but of men; so that many millions of people, and probably mostly of children, in an instant of time, at the dark, silent hour of midnight, were struck by the Angel of Death.

And the heart of Pharoah was again hardened, and his great army was led into the Red sea, and were drowned. While the Israelites were in the wilderness they were rebellious and disobedient; so the Lord sent fire to consume them, serpents to bite; and even opened the earth, and crushed them in its crevices.   And he kept them in the wilderness until six hundred thousand men of war had died; and with the aged men, and the women and children that also died, during their forty years of wanderings, the total number that died and were buried in the desert sands was probably not less than two millions.

And when the warriors of Israel, over a half million strong, under the leadership and with the assistance of the Lord of Hosts, swarmed into Canaan, attacked and destroyed over three score cities, and killed all the inhabitants thereof, men, women and children, can any estimate be formed of the millions upon millions of human beings cut off in their sins?

And we must not forget that not only these had died without warning, but that the entire world was, and had always been, and would continue to be until the coming of the

Savior, in a condition of midnight darkness as to any revelation regarding a future state of existence.

And we are not aware that any particular code of laws was given by the Lord for the observance of man until that given to the Hebrews, twenty-five hundred years after the creation of man. And this was made applicable only to them; so that all the rest of the world was left without any moral laws of any kind.

All the penalties imposed under the Jewish code were of a physical and temporal nature; such as subjection and spoliation by enemies, failure of crops, and bodily afflictions.

No allusion, intelligible to even the Hebrews, was made regarding a heaven and a hell. These were the enshrouded mysteries that would remain such unto the coming of the one who would be the first to rise from the grave, and the herald of glad tidings to all men.

What then is the only reasonable conclusion? Is it not that as the Lord has made

himself known to only a few of the myriads
of mankind, the few chosen, selected ones to
whom he in his own mysterious way, revealed
himself and his will, and left all the remain-
der to live and die strangers to the living
God, so he would, in thus ordaining the few
unto eternal life, without merit on their part,
cast all the others aside with the rest of living,
sentient beings, to live and die, and be no
more forever?   This seems the only logical,
inevitable conclusion.

The potter makes vessels, some unto
honor, some unto dishonor.

Beginning with Seth and ending with the
calling of Abraham, a period of two thousand
years, there was no religious organization on
earth.   The Lord gave his laws and his
spirit to his own, individually, wherever they
might be.

With Abraham he began the first church;
and for the next two thousand years Abraham and his descendents, the twelve tribes
of Israel, with the Lord as the head, was the
only church, the only recipient and observer
of divine commands in all the world.

But this was now to be supplanted. The Lord would yield up his headship, and his church of the twelve tribes, unto his Son, the Christ, and his twelve apostles. A church of laws, of sacrifices and physical penalties, would give place to a church of faith, of spiritual influence and regeneration.

CHAPTER XII.

THE ADVENT OF JESUS, AND HIS TEMPTATIONS.

And now would be the beginning of the end.

To the circumstances and events now about to transpire pointed all the laws and the prophets.

From the death through Adam, down the long ages to the life through Christ, from the garden of Eden to the garden of Gethsemane, all events wherein was seen the hand of God, flowed in steady, unswerving currents to this grand terminal of full fruition.

As Cain, the first born of Eve, was the son of Satan, and brought in death, so Christ, the first born of Mary, was the son of the living God, and would bring the dead of the Lord to life again.

The coming of the Saviour was the solving of the great mystery of all past ages, the object of all types and symbols.

The forty days' rain of the flood, the three days of Egyptian darkness, the brazen serpent in the wilderness, were but types of his life and mission.

The earth reclaimed from its desolation, man created, and Satan loosed for a season, were the three primal steps leading up to this culmination of the Lord's grand design.

Satan was apparently victorious, but was always vanquished. He had beguiled Adam, had slain Abel, and corrupted the antediluvian world; and, after the flood, had the entire earth in his service. But what had he gained? The great Jehovah was guiding and shaping all to the accomplishment of his own designs. The destinies of nations, as of individuals, were in the hollow of his hand. He worked in the silent, mysterious, irresistable ways of Omnipotent power. He foresaw from the beginning, because he foreordained; and he foreordained, because all things in the universe being his by creation and maintenance, possess no inherent independent powers of their own, but would either instantly cease to exist without his

sustaining, guiding presence; or, as to immortal spirits, his omniscience and omnipotence utterly preclude the possibility of any,
thing being left to chance, or to the caprice
of finite creatures.

He is the great I Am, the first and the
last, the one only God of all.

In ages past the Lord had said by his
prophet : " Behold, a virgin shall conceive
and bear a son, and shall call his name Immanuel.   And the government shall be
upon his shoulders, and his name shall be
called wonderful counsellor, the Mighty God,
the Everlasting Father, the Prince of Peace."

" And the spirit of the Lord shall rest
upon him, the spirit of wisdom and understanding."

" And he shall stand for an ensign of the
people, to it shall the Gentiles seek; and his
rest shall be glorious."

The angel Gabriel was sent from God
unto a city of Gallilee named Nazareth.

To a virgin espoused to a man whose
name was Joseph of the house of David; and
the virgin's name was Mary.

And the angel came in unto her and said: " Hail, thou that are highly favored, the Lord is with thee; blessed are thou amongst women."

And when she saw him she was troubled at his saying and cast in her mind what manner of salutation this should be.

And the angel said unto her: " Fear not, Mary; for thou hast found favor with the Lord. And behold thou shalt conceive in thy womb and bring forth a son, and shall call his name Jesus."

" He shall be great, and shall be called the Son of the Highest, and the Lord God shall give unto him the throne of his father, David."

" And He shall reign over the house of Jacob for ever, and of His kingdom there shall be no end."

Then said Mary unto the angel: " How shall this be, seeing I know not a man?"

And the angel answered and said unto her: "The Holy Ghost shall come upon thee and the power of the Highest shall over shadow thee; therefore, also that holy thing which shall be born of thee shall be called the Son of God."

"And behold thy cousin Elizabeth, she hath also conceived a son in her old age; and this is the sixth month with her who was called barren. For with God nothing shall be impossible."

And Mary said, "Behold, the handmaid of the Lord—be it unto me according to thy word." And the angel departed from her.

And it came to pass that Joseph and Mary went up into Bethlehem of Judea to be taxed.

And while they were there the days were accomplished that she should be delivered.

And she brought forth her first born and wrapped him in swaddling clothes, and laid him in a manger; for there was no room for them in the inn.

And there were in the same country shepherds abiding in the field, keeping watch over their flocks by night.

And lo, the angel of the Lord came upon them, and the glory of the Lord shone round about them, and they were sore afraid. And the angel said unto them: " Fear not, for behold I bring you good tidings of great joy, which shall be to all people."

" For unto you is born this day in the city of David a Saviour, which is Christ the Lord."

" And this shall be a sign unto you. Ye shall find the babe wrapped in swaddling clothes, lying in a manger." And suddenly there was with the angel a multitude of the heavenly host praising God and saying:

"Glory to God in the highest, and on earth peace, good will toward men."

And the child grew and waxed strong in spirit, filled with wisdom, and the grace of God was upon him; and he increased in wisdom and stature, and in favor with God and man.

There is mention of only one incident in the life of Jesus until he was thirty years of age.

When he was twelve years old he was for several days in the temple of Jerusalem talking with the priests; was with them asking and answering questions. And his knowledge and understanding excited wonder.

He then returned home with his parents, remaining with them until he entered upon his ministry.

He may have been educated in the ordinary learning of that day, and no doubt was. His reputed father, Joseph, was a carpenter of ordinary means; and though there is mention of Jesus reading in the synagogue, nothing is said of his ever having written anything at any time.

But he had all the human learning that was necessary, and whether it was acquired or bestowed is immaterial.

Human learning and knowledge, beyond a very limited point, add nothing to happiness, and very seldom fail to do injury. It takes so little to make men proud and vain, that much learning has an effect like riches, in disqualifying for pure and humble thought, and unquestioning obedience.

John came as a forerunner of the Saviour, warning the people that the Messiah was at hand, charging them to repent of all their wickedness and be baptized with water, as a token of purification, and of initiation into a new order, a new kingdom.

The baptism of John was an order from the King of kings, and was preparatory to the incoming of the Son; was the first step in setting aside the Jewish church, a church of blood, for the new one in which the sins of the people would be washed away as by water.

And Jesus went also and was baptized by John, in fulfillment of the law, and as an induction into his kingdom.

And as he came up from the baptism, the spirit of God, in the form of a dove, descended and rested on him, and a voice was heard saying: '' This is my beloved Son, in whom I am well pleased."

And immediately after, the spirit led him into the wilderness to be tempted of the devil.

And after he had fasted forty days and forty nights he was ahungered, and Satan appeared to tempt him.

He tempted him to show his power as the Son of God, by turning stones into bread to satisfy his hunger—to throw himself from a pinnacle of the temple—and lastly, from a high mountain, where could be seen vast kingdoms and glittering palaces of royalty; all of these he offered him, all the kingdoms of the world, if he would only fall down and worship him.

Satan thus appealed to probably the three strongest feelings of the human heart—appetite, pride and ambition.

In Satan thus tempting Jesus may there not be more things suggested than we have been willing to admit?

Satan had tempted Adam, and he fell; had tempted thousands of others—Moses, Aaron, David, Solomon—yea, millions of men, and all had sinned. Even he himself, and his angels, had been tempted through pride, and had fallen beyond redemption.

But all these, and himself, and all the angels of light, were finite creatures, with allegiance due the King of Heaven.

Is it not almost certain that he thought Jesus was of no superior type?

Had Satan known that Jesus was the very Son of the great King, was an emanation from, a part of the spirit of God, would he not have known that he could not be tempted? That as Son and Heir of the Father all the world was his already, and to him all things were possible?

And if he did not know, is it not an authorized inference that with the advent of Jesus began the separate existence of the Son of God?

From the very beginning and throughout the entire Revelation of the Lord, the idea of oneness is conveyed. And whenever any allusion is made to any thing resembling a separation, it is a sending forth of His spirit for some designated purpose—and even then it appears not so much a distinct individuality, as a reaching forth of an indivisible portion of an all pervading presence.

But with the birth of Jesus there seemed to be an actual separation from the one God and His spirit, the Holy Ghost, of a portion of their infinite spirit, and incarnating it with the body and blood of man.

And in this union of mortality and immortality, Son of man and Son of God,

Jesus was unknown to Satan—unknown and incorruptable.

Is not the theme of redemption inconceivably more grand on the plan of this conception?

There is not created another Prince, with a host of angels, to take the place of the great rebel and his legions; but the very Son of his Sovereign Lord, and Son of the man whom he had seduced to rebellion, will succeed him, not only as Prince, but as King and Judge.

After Satan had departed from tempting Jesus, angels came and ministered to him. He then returned from the wilderness, and going forth into Gallilee and elsewhere, met and called his twelve disciples who were to remain with him during his three years of ministry. He did not select from the priests —nor from the learned—nor from those in high places—but he chose fishermen and others in the humble walks of life—whose faith would be strong, whose convictions deep and lasting.

And for three years he went through

Judea and the country round about, preaching righteousness and obedience to God; healing the sick, and casting out devils. For the devils knew him now—knew him as the Son of God, and with power to punish them.

But it is not evident that they understood that he was first to die and be raised from death before his mission was finished. For it was Satan himself that entered into Judas Iscariot and induced him to betray his master unto death, which he certainly would not have done had he known that he was carrying out the plans of the Lord that were designed to end in his own eternal discomfiture.

The doctrine that Jesus taught was clear, simple, easy to understand. It was only to believe that he was the Son of God, and to live a pure life.

His mission was nearly finished. He had kept unto himself all that his Father had given him, and the end drew near.

CHAPTER XIII.

HIS MINISTRY, TRIAL AND CONDEMNATION.

There is one peculiar characteristic in the entire history of the Saviour that is worthy of profound consideration—and that is, the quiet, undemonstrative nature of all its incidents.

The conception was known to only four persons—the parents of Jesus and of John. Or, if to others, to only a few of their relatives. And his birth was not even at his mother's home, but at the house of a stranger —and not even in the house proper, but in a stable or manger of the inn.

The announcement of this most glorious event was made only to a few shepherds who were attending their flocks by night, and who hurried to the inn to do homage to the new born Immanuel. When he was taken into the temple to be circumcised, the high priest knew that he was the Son of God, as did also an aged prophetess who was there, but none others seem to have known. But it must at least have been talked about to have reached the ears of Herod, probably through the inquiries of the shepherds; and he, becoming alarmed at the probability of there being a claimant to the throne of King David, sent forth his soldiers, and killed all the male children that were two years old and under, throughout Bethlehem and all the coasts thereof, expecting in that way to certainly slay the reputed claimant.

After the return of Joseph and Mary from Egypt, whither they had fled from Herod, and their settlement in Nazareth, the life of Jesus seems to have been as simple, unobtrusive and unnoted as that of any young man of the day.

When entering on his ministry, he provided no worldly means of any kind, had no abiding place, no place where to lay his head.

And as he went over all Judea and the neighboring districts, calling sinners to repentance, and performing his wonderful miracles, there was no change in his bearing. He spoke as one having authority, as knowing the truth of his words, the faithfulness of his promises, but his language was simple and plain, his voice low and gentle, his every act kind and compassionate.

He exercised no dictatorial rule over his disciples, but was to them more like an elder brother than a master; instructing them in the ways of righteousness, and admonishing them when in error.

The human mind could never have conceived a being of such attributes as was Jesus of Nazareth.

He was the Son of God, yet the very embodiment of gentleness and of loving kindness.

He never refused a favor asked, and never was a prayer unheard.

He even shed tears over the sufferings of others, tears of sympathy, tears that showed he had feelings like other men,— human feelings, that could suffer pain, could moan and weep.

He seemed not so much to fear and

deprecate the punishment of the wicked, as to have a deep, abiding love for his disciples, and for all those that would come unto him; a love that promised, not temporal blessings and pleasures, but a mansion in his Father's house.

And with what infinite love and reverence he always spoke of his Father; even as a dependent, loving child that never questioned and never had a doubt. All honor, all glory was due the Father, and obedience even unto death. A sin against the Son could be forgiven, but against the Father, or his Holy Spirit, never; neither in this world, nor in the world to come.

And as the Son loved the Father, even so the Father loved the Son, and had his angels guarding his every step.

The entrance of Jesus into Jerusalem was consistent with what had gone before.

He drew near and entered the city where was the temple of his Father, not in a chariot of state and clothed in fine attire, but as a tired, weary traveler, poorly and humbly clad, and riding on an ass.

He ate the passover supper with his disciples, the last with them on earth; in a chamber by themselves. He talked with them and explained many things that he wished them to understand, and gave them his final instructions. And he took a basin of water and a towel and washed their feet, as an example unto them.

And he took bread and gave thanks and broke it and gave it unto them and said, "Eat, this is my body, which is given for you." And he took the cup and blessed it, and gave it to them, saying, "Drink ye all of it, for this is my blood of the new testament, which is shed for many, for the remission of sins."

And Judas Iscariot, Satan having entered into him, went out to betray his master.

And Jesus and his disciples went forth, and it was night, and they came into the mount of Olives.

"Then cometh Jesus with them unto a place called Gethsemane, and saith unto his disciples, "Sit ye here while I go and pray yonder."

And he took with him Peter, and the two sons of Zebedee, and began to be sorrowful and very heavy.

And he went a little farther, and fell on his face and prayed, saying, "Oh, my Father, if it be possible, let this cup pass from me; nevertheless, not as I will, but as thou wilt."

And there appeared an angel unto him from heaven, strengthening him.

And being in an agony, he prayed more earnestly; and his sweat was, as it were, great drops of blood falling down to the ground.

And when he rose from prayer and was come to his disciples, he found them sleeping.

And immediately a multitude appeared, and Judas, one of the twelve, went before them, and drew near unto Jesus to kiss him. But Jesus said unto him, "Judas, betrayest thou the Son of man with a kiss?"

And when Simon Peter drew his sword and cut off an ear of a servant of the priest, Jesus chided him, and put forth his hand and healed the ear.

And they took Jesus before the high

priest and mocked him, and a servant of the priest even struck him. And they held a council to get ready their false testimony.

And when it was daylight they took Jesus unto the hall of judgement, and they themselves went not in, lest they should be defiled; but that they might eat the passover.

Pilate then went out unto them and said: "What accusation bring ye against this man?"

They answered and said unto him, "If he were not a malefactor, we would not have delivered him up unto thee." Then said Pilate unto them, "Take ye him, and judge him according to your law." The Jews, therefore, said unto him, "It is not lawful for us to put any man to death."

Then Pilate entered unto the judgement hall again, and called Jesus, and said unto him, "Art thou the King of the Jews?"

Jesus answered him, "Sayest thou this thing of thyself, or did others tell it thee of me?"

Pilate answered, "Am I a Jew? Thine own nation, and the chief priests, have delivered thee unto me.   What hast thou done?"

Jesus answered, " My kingdom is not of this world; if my kingdom were of this world, then would my servants fight that I should not be delivered to the Jews; but now is my kingdom not from hence."

And Pilate, being desirous to release Jesus, for his wife had sent unto him saying, " Have nothing to do with that just man, for I have suffered many things this day in a dream because of him," went again out to the Jews and said unto them, "I find in him no fault at all."

" But ye have a custom that I should release unto you one at the passover; will ye, therefore, that I release unto you the King of the Jews?"

Then cried they all saying, "Not this man, but Barabbas."   Now, Barabbas was a robber and a murderer.   Then Pilate took Jesus and scourged him.   And the soldiers platted a crown of thorns and put it on his head, and they put on him a purple robe, and in his hand a reed, and said, "Hail, King of the Jews," and they smote him with their hands.

Pilate went forth again unto the Jews, and saith unto them, "Behold, I bring him forth to you, that ye may know that I find no fault with him." Then came Jesus forth wearing the crown of thorns and the purple robe.

And Pilate saith unto them, "Behold the man."

When the chief priests and officers saw him, they cried out, "Crucify him, crucify him." Pilate saith unto them, "Take ye him and crucify him, for I find no fault in him." The Jews answered him, "We have a law, and by our law he ought to die, because he made himself the Son of God." When Pilate heard that saying, he was the more afraid, and went again unto the judgement hall, and saith unto Jesus, "Whence art thou?" But Jesus gave him no answer.

Then saith Pilate unto him, "Speakest thou not unto me: knowest thou not that I have power to crucify thee, and have power to release thee?" Jesus answered, "Thou couldst have no power at all against me, except it were given thee from above; therefore, he that delivered me unto thee hath the greater sin."

And from thenceforth Pilot sought to release him; but the Jews cried out saying, "If thou let this man go, thou art not Cesar's friend; whoever maketh himself a king speaketh against Cesar."

When Pilate heard that he brought Jesus forth and sat down in the judgement seat in a place that is called (in the Hebrew) Gabbatha.

And it was the preparation of the passover, and about the sixth hour; and he said unto the Jews, "Behold your king!" But they cried out, "Away with him, away with him; crucify him."

Pilate saith unto them, "Shall I crucify your king?" The chief priests answered, "We have no king but Cesar."

And when Pilate saw that he could prevail nothing, but that rather a tumult was made, he took water and washed his hands before the multitude, saying, "I am innocent of the blood of this just person, see ye to it." Then answered all the people and said,

" His blood be on us, and our children."

Then delivered he him unto them to be crucified, and they took Jesus and led him away.

CHAPTER XIV.

HIS DEATH, RESURRECTION AND ASCENSION.

And as they led him away they laid hold upon one Simeon, a Cyrenian, coming out of the country, and on him they laid the cross, that he might bear it with Jesus.

And when they come to the place, which is called Calvary, there they crucified him; and also the two malefactors, one on the right hand and the other on the left; and Jesus said, "Father, forgive them, for they know not what they do."

And they set up over his head his accusation, written "Jesus of Nazareth, the King of the Jews."

And they that passed by reviled him, wagging their heads, and saying, "Thou that destroyest the temple, and buildest it in three days, save thyself. If thou be the Son of God, come down from the cross." Likewise also the chief priests mocking him, with

the scribes and elders said, " He saved others, himself he cannot save.   He trusted in
God; let him deliver him now if he will have
him; for he said, ' I am the Son of God.'"

And one of the malefactors railed on
him, but the other said, "Lord, remember
me when thou comest into thy kingdom;
and Jesus said unto him, "Verily I say
unto thee, to-day shalt thou be with me in
paradise."

Then the four soldiers that had crucified
him, took his garments and made four parts
—to every soldier a part; except his coat,
which was without seam, woven from the
top throughout—for that they cast lots.

And it was about the sixth hour that
they crucified him, and there was darkness
over all the earth until the ninth hour.

And about the ninth hour Jesus cried
with a loud voice, saying, " My God, why
hast thou forsaken me."   And then he said,
" I thirst."   And one of them ran and took
a sponge and filled it with vinegar, and put
it on a reed and put it to his mouth.   When
Jesus had received the vinegar, he said, "It

is finished; Father, into thy hands I commend my spirit." And having said thus, he gave up the ghost.

And, behold, the vail of the temple was rent in twain from the top to the bottom; and the earth did quake, and the rocks were rent.

The Jews, therefore, because it was the preparation, that the bodies should not remain upon the cross on the Sabbath day, besought Pilate that their legs might be broken, and they might be taken away. Then came the soldiers and brake the legs of the first, and of the other which was crucified with him. But when they came to Jesus, and saw that he was dead already, they brake not his legs; but one of the soldiers with a spear pierced his side, and forthwith came thereout blood and water.

And after this, Joseph of Arimathea got leave from Pilate and took the body of Jesus. And there came also Nicodemus, and brought a mixture of myrrh and aloes, about a hundred pounds weight. Then took they the body of Jesus and wound it in linen clothes with the spices, as the manner of the Jews is to bury.

There was a garden in the place where he was crucified, and in the garden a new sepulcher, hewn out in the rock, wherein was never man yet laid. There laid they Jesus, for the sepulcher was nigh at hand.

And they rolled a great stone to the door of the sepulcher and departed.

Now, the next day the chief priests and pharisees came together unto Pilate and said, " Sir, we remember that that deceiver said while he was yet alive, 'After three days I will arise again.'

"Command, therefore, that the sepulcher be made sure until the third day, lest his disciples come by night and steal him away, and say unto the people, ' He is risen from the dead;' so the last error shall be worse than the first." Pilate said unto them, " Ye have a watch, go your way, make it as sure as you can."

So they went and made the sepulcher sure, sealing the stone, and setting a watch.

And as it began to dawn towards the

first day of the week, came Mary Magdalene, and the other Mary to see the sepulcher.

And behold there was a great earthquake; for the angel of the Lord descended from heaven, and came and rolled back the stone from the door, and sat upon it.

His countenance was like lightning, and his raiment white as snow. And the keepers did shake and become as dead men.

And the angel said unto the women, "Fear not ye; for I know that ye seek Jesus, which was crucified. He is not here; for he is risen, as he said.

"Come, see the place where the Lord lay.

"And go quickly, and tell his disciples that he is risen from the dead, and behold, he goeth before you unto Galilee; there shall ye see see him; lo, I have told you."

And they ran and told Peter and John, and these came running with Mary and went into the sepulcher, and seeth the linen clothes lie, and the napkin lying together in a place by itself. They did not yet know the scripture, that he must rise again from the dead.

After Jesus had risen from the dead he appeared to his disciples several different times. Once when the eleven, and some others, were gathered together in Jerusalem, Jesus stood in the midst of them, and saith unto them, ''Peace be unto you." But they were terrified and afrighted, and supposed that they had seen a spirit. And he saith unto them, "Why are ye troubled? And why do thoughts arise in your hearts? Behold my hands and my feet, that it is I myself; handle me, and see, for a spirit hath not flesh and bones, as ye see me have." And he showed them his hands and his feet. And while they yet believed not for joy, and wondered, he said unto them, " Have ye here any meat?" And they gave him a piece of a broiled fish and of a honey comb. And he took it and did eat before them.

And then he talked with them, and opened their understanding that they might understand the scriptures, and said unto them, "Thus it is written, and thus it behooved Christ to suffer, and to rise from the dead the third day."

"And that repentance and remission of sins should be preached in his name among all nations, beginning at Jerusalem. And ye are witnesses of these things."

"And behold I send the promise of my Father upon you; but tarry ye in the City of Jerusalem until ye be endowed with power from on high."

And he led them out as far as the Beth-amy; and he lifted up his hands and blessed them.

And it came to pass while he blessed them he was parted from them, and carried up into heaven.

And they worshipped him, and returned to Jerusalem with great joy.

Thus ended the most sad, the most tragic scenes ever enacted on earth.

The Son of God, and true heir to the throne of David, rejected by his own people; and by the priests and rulers in the temple of his own Father was he persecuted, mocked, spat upon, and at last crucified between two thieves. He was led as a lamb to the slaughter, but not by these whited

sepulchers themselves.   Their hypocritical
sanctity would not even permit their entrance
into the judgment hall, where their master
was being tried for his life on their own accu-
sations; but they urged and strengthened
the hands of idolators, of the servants of the
Devil, to commit the sacreligious deed.   And
when that humane heathen, Pilate, remon-
strated with them, they cried out the more
fiercely, "Crucify him, crucify him—on us
and our children be his blood."

Could madness go farther?   Could fanat-
icism, bigotry, intolerance be possibly more
pliant tools for Satan?

And speedily came their punishment.
The sword of God's vengeance was un-
sheathed, their blood and the blood of their
children was spilled like water; their land
was left desolate, and as a hunted, persecuted race were they scattered amongst all
the nations of the earth.

Though they were the instruments of
God, their blood guiltiness was none the
less.

And it is one of the deep mysteries of

God that his church, his only church, his own people, chosen and adopted midst signs and wonders and great miracles, should be selected as such instrument; and thereafter should be, as it were, spewed from the mouth forever.

For their eyes have ever been blinded, and their hearts hardened even unto this day.

And though their crime was most heinous, the fruits thereof were glorious and immediate.

For when the angel descended and loosed the seals, and rolled the stone from the mouth of the sepulcher, there was a great earthquake, and as Jesus walked forth, the first to rise from the dead, other graves were opened, others came up from death to life,—thousands of them, tens of thousands, and ascended with Christ to reign with him unto the second resurrection and final judgment.

When Jesus came from the tomb he forbade anyone to touch him until he had ascended to God.

He returned again to earth, and when he

ascended again and finally, it may have been to the throne of the Father, into the profound depths of illimitable space; or it may have been to some planet of his kingdom; to the Sun, the great, glorious central orb of our system of worlds; or it may have been to Venus, the star of the morning, the bright harbinger of day; or to Saturn, or to brilliant Jupiter. Any one, or more, of these may have been purified and made ready for the millenium, where Christ and his saints could reign until time ceased, and the earth was also made suitable for the abode of God's elect.

We cannot consider this unreasonable or improbable. Nothing is impossible with God. The idea of an earthly millenium is in the highest degree chimerical, and is without warrant of scripture.

With the advent of Christ, the Devil and his angels were chained. They never disputed his authority over them, his power and right to cast them out of men. And when his disciples had received the Holy Ghost, and started on their mission, they went possessed of the like power to cast out devils and heal all diseases. The control over evil spirits, by driving them from man, is the only chaining probably meant. Or if there were any other meaning, it is hidden from us, and always will be.

It is quite certain that since the beginning of the Christian era, Satan and his legions have been no less active, persistent, and successful in their efforts than they were previously.

Anti-Christs came, and with such show of genuineness, that, had it been possible, even the elect would have been deceived. All form of opposition, of distortion, of corruption, were ever resorted to.

During the lives of the apostles the churches that they had established were kept compartively pure; for the Holy Spirit was with them, as Jesus had promised. But when they had gone to their rest, when miracles had ceased, the churches gradually drew farther and farther away from the true teachings of Christ, until after a few centuries had passed, there was not in all the earth, probably, even one that held the true doctrine, that was anything more than a hollow mockery of the great original. Where was the church at Jerusalem? at Corinth? in Thessaly? at Rome? Did any of these teach the doctrines of their Head and King? Had they not drifted, or rather been led by Satan, into the vanities, vices and corruptions of the times?

The great red dragon was speedily getting control, complete, thorough possession of the church of Christ as established by the apostles; and would hold it unto the end.

But this also was a part of the plan of the Lord of all the earth. The good seed was sown, had taken root throughout the world, and the Spirit of the Lord would watch over his elect. The shepherd knows his sheep, they know his voice, and not one will be left out of the fold.

CHAPTER XV.

THE ANTI-CHRIST; THE JUDGMENT; THE NEW KINGDOM.

The last sacrifice had been offered; the paschal lamb, without blemish, as in the land of Egypt. Its blood had been drawn, as there, only the application was different. Christ gave them the bread, it was his body; he gave them the wine, it was his blood. Not a bone was broken; and the body was not kept till morning, but was hid in the sepulchre. Now, as then, death came not where the blood was; but then, it was the death averted for the time only; while now, if averted, it would be for all eternity. It was the final, all-sufficient sacrifice. There would be no further use for an earthly temple, so it was shaken and rocked to its foundation; no more use for a vail to hide its holy mysteries, so it was rent in twain from top to bottom. Now and henceforth the hearts of his elect would be his temple, and the dwelling place of his Holy Spirit.

In looking over the past, there are two numerals and their multiples, that attract attention and incite wonder, by their frequent occurrence in all the important events of the world's history. And they are the numbers three and forty.

The creation of the world occupied twice three days, or periods; there were three persons in the garden of Eden; the flood lasted three times fifty days; the earth was peopled by the three sons of Noah; the Egyptian darkness lasted three days. And nearly all the incidents in the life, trial and death of the Saviour occupied three hours, three days, three years, or multiples of three.

Even his final church will be the third. The Jewish was vacated and set aside; that the apostles founded and that was finally seated at Rome, was abandoned and disowned; the third and last will be the eternal church, pure, undefiled, and unchangeable.

We can well understand that three is typical of the trinity of the Godhead. But the numeral forty has also a symbolic meaning which is to us unknown. At the flood it rained forty days; Moses was in the mount forty days; the Jews in the wilderness for forty years; Christ in the wilderness forty days. Must we not feel quite certain that these repetitions of that numeral point to some definite subject, or to some existing objects?

It may have reference to the number of the planets and their satelites, that constituted the principalities and powers of the lost kingdom of Satan, and that will be the reclaimed kingdom of Christ, the new heaven and the new earth.

And are we not justified in thinking that these types will be carried still farther? There was one period of two thousand years —fifty times forty—from Adam to Abraham; a second of two thousand from Abraham to the coming of the Son of God; a third of two thousand, to the end of all finite things; and being also a thousand years for each of the six days of creation.

Prophecies, however clear in their gen-

eral import, were never so as to details, nor
to the determining of the times of their fulfil-
ment. It was well understood that the Lord
would send the house of Israel a king, and
that the temple would be destroyed: and so
is it now known that the world will at last
be consumed with fire, and time be no more.
But the prophetic seven weeks, and sixty
and two weeks; and the time, and times and
half times, convey no definite idea of the
actually set time.

But with typical numbers it is different;
they are, from their very nature, determinate
and invariable.

In the twentieth century there will be
such a culmination in the combining of the
mystic numbers three and forty, that we are
impressed with the conviction that it will be
the final one, and will witness the closing
scenes of time. The three times fifty days
of the flood will have been again shown in
three parts, in the fifty times forty years,
making a total of one hundred and fifty
times forty years, ending with the year
2000 A. D.

The twentieth century, the closing one of the third, and no doubt final great epoch, begins with the year 1901.

It may be that the end will come in its third typical forty, which begins with 1961.

We feel also assured that the number of the Christ, and the number of the anti-Christ, will enter into the final combination.

AND 3 TIMES 666 ARE 1998.

We can reflect, can consider, but not even the angels of God know the time appointed for the end.

The sowers of the good seed have gone throughout the world, and some has fallen in good ground and brought forth abundantly. The heralds of the Messiah have called forth from mountain and valley, from city and hamlet, the glad tidings of great joy, and the chosen of God have hearkened to the call.

The words of the Savior come echoing down from century to century: "Come unto me, all ye that labor and are heavy laden, and I will give you rest. I am the way and the life; he that believeth on me and doeth my works, shall never die. Come, drink of the water of life freely; for it is given without price, and floweth from the throne of thy God. Come to the marriage feast of the Lamb that was slain from the foundation of the world."

In all nations, under all skies, are found the children of the kingdom; few in number, perchance, and to the world unknown; meek and lowly, persecuted and downtrodden; but God dwelleth in their hearts, and for them there is a mansion in their Father's house. And for them was the prayer of the Son of God when with his disciples, "Father, I pray not for the world, but for these that thou has given me, and for those that shall believe on me through their word." They are the wheat that shall be garnered at the last day.

But the despoiler is abroad; the prince of all evil has never ceased his unrelenting warfare against the elect of God.

Driving the followers of Christ from Jerusalem with persecution and violence, he followed them elsewhere; and when not oppressing and killing, he sought to deceive and corrupt.

And soon he succeeded, not in destroying, but in getting under his control, the very church itself. It was but a few hundred years until his followers, now priests, bishops and popes, assumed all the rights, privileges and prerogatives of God himself. They claimed to hold the keys of heaven and hell; they could release souls from purgatory, a mitigated hell of their own invention, and send them up to heaven on angels' wings; they could enthrone and dethrone the kings of the earth; they could take their sinful fellow men, and, declaring them saints, hold them up before their deluded followers as objects of worship.

They even worshipped the mother of Jesus, and prayed unto her, rather than unto the Son. And they had idols of various kinds, images, relics of the apostles, of the cross, of their so-called saints; and in every way corrupted themselves. And they did these things at the command of their head,

the pope, who claimed to be infallible and incapable of sin.   And not only did they thus
with themselves, but, instigated and moved
by Satan, the very anti-Christ-in-chief, they
persecuted the servants of God; they impris-
oned them; they tortured them with incon-
ceivable malignity; they cursed them with all
the anathemas of devils; they burned them;
they sawed them asunder; they flayed them
alive; until the whole world was red with the
blood of the saints, the chosen of God.

And there was war in heaven; Michael
and his angels fought against the dragon;
and the great dragon was cast out, the old
serpent, called the Devil, and Satan; he was
cast out into the earth and his angels were
cast out with him.

Woe to the inhabitants of the earth, for
the Devil is come down unto you, having
great wrath, because he knoweth he hath but
a short time.

And I saw a beast rise out of the sea
(from the flood, where were drowned the

wicked offspring of Cain, and the other Sons of God), having seven heads and ten horns, and upon his horns ten crowns, and upon his head the name of blasphemy. And I saw one of his heads as it were wounded unto death; and his deadly wound was healed. And they worshipped the dragon which gave power unto the beast. And there was given unto him a mouth speaking great things and blasphemies, and power was given unto him to continue forty and two months, (of such number was the generations from Adam unto to the coming of the Saviour; as also was the temple of God to be trodden under foot of the Gentiles). And all that dwell upon the earth shall worship this beast whose names are not written in the book of life.

And I beheld another beast coming up out of the earth, and he had two horns, like a lamb, and he spake as a dragon (this is the anti-Christ that takes the church of the Lamb of God, and causeth the earth to wor-ship the first beast whose wound was healed).

And he doth great wonders, so that he maketh fire to come down from heaven; and he deceived by his miracles, and had the dwellers on earth make an image of the beast, and he gave life unto the image, so that it could both speak and cause those to be killed who would not worship it. And he caused all, great and small, to receive his mark in their right hand, or in their foreheads; and this mark was 666.

And I looked, and lo, a lamb stood on Mount Zion, and with him a hundred and forty-four thousand, having his father's name written in their foreheads. These were redeemed from amongst men, being the first fruits unto God and to the Lamb.

And I saw another angel in the midst of heaven, having the everlasting gospel to preach unto them that dwell on the earth.

And there followed another angel, saying, Babylon is fallen, is fallen.

And a third angel followed, saying with a loud voice, If any man worship the beast and his image, and receive his mark in his forehead, or in his hand, the same shall drink of the wine of the wrath of God, and shall be tormented with fire and brimstone, and the smoke of their torment ascendeth up forever and ever.

An angel said unto me, Come hither; I will show unto thee the judgment of the great whore that setteth upon many waters.

And I saw a woman sit upon a scarlet colored beast, full of names of blasphemy, having seven heads and ten horns. And the woman was arrayed in purple and scarlet color, and decked with gold and precious stones. And upon her forehead was a name written: MYSTERY. BABYLON THE GREAT. THE MOTHER OF HARLOTS AND ABOMINATIONS OF THE EARTH.' And I saw the woman drunken with the blood of the saints, and with the blood of the martyrs of Jesus.

And the angel said, I will tell thee the mystery of the woman, and of the beast that carrieth her, which hath the seven heads and the ten horns. The beast that was, and is not, and yet is, shall ascend out of the bottomless pit. The seven heads are seven mountains, on which the woman sitteth; and the ten horns are ten kings, who shall receive power one hour with the beast; and the waters where the whore sitteth are peoples and multitudes, and nations and tongues.

And the ten horns which thou sawest upon the beast, these shall hate the whore, and shall make her desolate and naked, and shall eat her flesh, and burn her with fire. For God hath put in their hearts to fulfill his will, and to agree, and give their kingdom unto the beast until the words of God shall be fulfilled.

And I saw another angel, and he cried with a loud voice, Babylon, the great, is fallen, and is become the habitation of devils, and the hold of every foul spirit. And another voice cried, Come out of her, my people, that ye be not partakers of her sins; for her sins have reached unto heaven, and she shall be utterly burned with fire; for by her sorceries were all nations deceived; and in her was found the blood of prophets, and of saints, and of all that were slain upon the earth.

And the Lord God hath judged the great whore, which did corrupt the earth, and hath avenged the blood of his servants at her hand.

And her smoke rose up forever and ever.

And I saw heaven opened, and behold, a white horse, and he that sat upon him was called Faithful and True. His eyes were a flame of fire, and on his head were many crowns, and he had a name written that no man knew but himself. And he was clothed with a vesture dipped in blood; and on his vesture and on his thigh a name written, King of Kings, and Lord of Lords.

And the armies which were in heaven followed him upon white horses, clothed in fine linen, white and clean.

And I saw an angel standing in the sun, and he cried with a loud voice, saying to all the fowls that fly, Come unto the supper of the great God, that ye may eat the flesh of kings, and the flesh of captains, and the flesh of mighty men, and the flesh of horses, and of them that sit on them, and the flesh of all men, both free and bond, both small and great.

And I saw the beast, and the kings of

the earth, and their armies gathered together to make war against him that sat on the horse, and against his army.

And the beast was taken, and with him the false prophet that wrought miracles that deceived those who received the mark of the beast, and that worshipped his image. These both were cast alive into a lake of fire burning with brimstone. And the remnant were slain with the sword of him that sat upon the horse, and all the fowls were filled with their flesh.

And the Devil was cast into the lake of fire where the beast and false prophet are, and shall be tormented day and night forever.

And I saw a great white throne and him that sat on it, from whose face the earth and the heaven fled away; and there was found no place for them.

And I saw the dead, small and great, stand before God; and the books were opened; and another book was opened, the book of life; and the dead were judged out of those things which were written in the books, according to their works.

And death and hell were cast into the lake of fire. And whoever was not found written in the book of life was cast into the lake of fire. This is the second death.

And I saw a new heaven and a new earth; for the first heaven and the first earth were passed away; and there was no more sea.

And I heard a great voice out of heaven saying, Behold, the tabernacle of God is with men, and he will dwell with them, and they shall be his people, and God himself shall be with them, and be their God. And there shall be no more death, nor sorrow, nor crying, nor any more pain; for the former things are passed away.

Behold, I make all things new.

And the angel carried me away in the spirit to a great and high mountain, and showed me that great city, the holy Jerusalem, descending out of heaven from God, having the glory of God, and her light was like unto a stone most precious, clear as crystal. And I saw no temple therein, for the Lord God almighty and the Lamb are the temple of it. And the city had no need of the sun, for the glory of God did lighten it, and the Lamb is the light thereof; and his servants shall serve him, and they shall see his face; and his name shall be in their foreheads, and they shall reign forever.

And he said unto me, These sayings are faithful and true. Behold, I come quickly. I am Alpha and Omega, the beginning and the end, the first and the last.

Blessed are they that do his commandments, that they may have right to the tree of life, and may enter in through the gates into the city.

Thus will be vindicated the power and the majesty of the God of the universe.

Thus will he finally and forever conquer Satan and his legions of fallen angels, and chain them in the lake of fire and brimstone for all eternity.

Thus will he consume with fire and purify from corruption, the old earth and the old heaven, and resurrect them into a new, pure, and perfect abode for the redeemed of the earth; those whom he created, built up, buried and resurrected again according to his own will.

And the ruler thereof will not be, as before, an angel, a finite being who fell through pride; but he will be his own beloved Son, the meek and lowly one of earth, who, as King and Lord, infinite as the Father in all his attributes, will reign with his saints forever and ever.

THE END.